# RENOVATION

## SARA BROOKE

# PROLOGUE

There was water everywhere.

In some places, it was dripping down from discolored patches on the ceiling. In other areas, it was sliding down the walls, landing on the windowsills, and splashing onto nearby furniture. The sound was maddening and constant. It seemed like an orchestra of destruction playing in stereo.

He thought he might go mad.

Everything was terribly wrong, and now his wife Jackie had left him for another man—left him in the shambles of what their home had once been.

Looking around at the peeling paint, torn flooring, and dripping ceiling, he knew that there was no choice. Despite all of the "eternal optimism" that he'd unluckily inherited from his mother, he could no longer hang on to the hope that things would turn out all right.

The renovation was a disaster. But there was something else too. Something he didn't want to think about because it made his head hurt, and it darkened the world, turning it cruel and angry.

Still, the thoughts were too loud to ignore, and the shouting inside of his mind rang from one lobe to the other.

*There is something wrong with them. They aren't normal. The way they look at me; the sounds I've been hearing. I'm not going crazy, am I? This isn't just a simple fuck up. There's something wrong.*

Just then, a piece of the vaulted ceiling came crashing down inches from his feet. The powdery drywall material surrounded him in a puff of white smoke, making him cough.

As he looked up, a gaping dark hole that had opened up into the attic stared back at him with a malevolent, jagged countenance.

He could see the rafters in the distance as they crisscrossed along the base of the roof, extending in opposite directions. It was strange to be staring at the underbelly of his home while he stood in his living room.

*Splat.*

"Shit," he muttered, wiping away the water that had fallen into his face and temporarily blinded his right eye. "I guess it's time to go."

He wasn't sure if he'd made the statement out loud or if it was just a phrase he'd formed in his mind. Either way, he was ready to walk away from an American dream that had turned into a nightmare of monumental proportions.

Suddenly, there was a response to his formidable statement. It was a breathy command, and one that seemed to emanate from every floorboard.

*No.*

"What the hell? Oh shit, I don't care what that was. I'm getting the fuck out of here."

He ran to the small table by the door—the one that had the metal plate he'd purchased with Jackie at the flea market. The one everyone thought was *such a steal*. The one Jackie had always joked would help keep him from forgetting his keys in the morning.

But right now, he couldn't stop to admire the ornate wonderment of the delicate plate. He just needed to get his keys, and get out of the cursed house.

Much to his relief, the keys were right where he'd left them and slid easily into his trembling hand. The feel of the cool metal against his palm was momentarily calming. However, when he pulled on the door, his nerves began jangling and everything went into high alert.

Because despite being unlocked, the door wouldn't open.

Or perhaps it was *refusing* to open.

In his panicked mind, he wondered if maybe the house was angry with him for all the abuse and destruction. Was it possible for an inanimate object to somehow, in the face of true evil, come to life?

And then, as if to confirm his wildest fears, the house began to compress and collapse into itself.

With mounting horror, he watched as the walls started closing in. It felt as if an earthquake was sending tremors throughout the four walls of the two-story home. Cracks began to appear along the floor, and more drywall tumbled to the ground as the air became increasingly hazy from the peeling paint and collapsing construction.

In the midst of the unbelievable, and through a haze of shock, he wondered if maybe he should run.

But there was no escape. He knew that now.

And when the ceiling fan dropped down and fatally hit him in the head, there was barely a sound. Just a thud as metal connected to flesh.

The real noise began when moments later, the entire roof fell to pieces, and the house shattered like projectile rocks hitting glass over and over again.

# 1

The scenery flew by the windshield in spurts of green and brown. Mikey wasn't sure how long they'd been driving because the hours seemed to meld together as their SUV traveled along a back road shortcut—thanks largely in part to the little GPS that was guiding them toward Northwest Florida.

The Brenniers weren't on a road trip. They were heading to their new life in Oak Shade, courtesy of Innovitran, Inc. After five months of frightening unemployment, Mikey had finally landed a job as a senior product engineer at an established medical device firm. However, Innovitran was geographically far away from Miami, so they were relocating to the relatively undiscovered town of Oak Shade.

Mikey knew that this move wasn't an exciting prospect for either his wife Barb or his 13-year-old son, Greg. He snuck a peek over at his less-than-enthused family members who were slumped in their respective seats, eyes closed, and mouths open as they both gently snored in unison. For a second, he felt a pang of guilt at having forced them into an unfamiliar part of the state where they'd have to make new friends and once again establish themselves.

Still, the new job would be paying quite well, and given the rough economic times, it wasn't like opportunity was exactly knocking on his door—so when a job like this one came about, compromises sometimes needed to be made.

He would also need to begin work straight away, giving him very little time to unpack and set up his home. According to the hiring manager at Innovitran, there was a significant set of product launches that needed his immediate attention, and so he'd agreed to start within days of arriving in town.

"Hey look, we're here." A tired voice from the backseat yanked Mikey out of his reverie. Greg was awake and staring out the window at a worn wooden sign that had been painted in bright greens and yellows.

*Welcome to Oak Shade. A family community.*

Mikey thought the sign was very quaint and felt his spirits rise as the rest of the town came into view. Despite being significantly smaller than their prior residence in West Miami, Oak Shade had character. The buildings and stores were neatly constructed, and people walked along the sidewalks in a leisurely manner. Some carried ice cream cones; others toted small bags of clothing or groceries.

It was like a scene out of a movie, and Mikey loved every minute of it. He'd always wanted to move somewhere that was slower paced than the busy city they'd grown accustomed to, and he was hoping that life in a smaller town would provide his family with a chance to become closer through activities like park picnics, celebrations, and more time spent with other families.

Mikey knew that he might be getting a bit idealistic in his old age, but the idea that something good could come out of an initial failure (his loss of employment in Miami) made him feel like everything was happening for a reason.

Hell, they were off to a good start anyway. He'd purchased a two-story Colonial-style home in a small neighborhood not far from Innovitran and was really looking forward to getting settled in.

*We'll all get used to our new life, and things will be fine. Everything happens for a reason.*

"Honey, are we almost there?" Barb stretched in her seat and yawned, taking a look out of the window for the first time since they'd left the main stretch of highway. "Wow, this place looks like it's right out of some 1950's movie," she mused, "Everything is so clean and safe-looking."

"Yeah, not like West Miami," Mikey replied with a hint of sarcasm. He originally hailed from Michigan and had never been a fan of the bustling South Florida scene. He preferred a slower pace where people knew each other, and families could leave their front doors unlocked without the fear of getting robbed.

"I liked Miami," Barb said, still looking out the window.

Mikey wasn't sure what to say. He knew that Barb, a Miami native wasn't thrilled about leaving everything behind. But he had to believe that this was the right move.

In his opinion, there was no going back.

———

Mikey slowed down, pulling his car up along the short gravel driveway that led up to their new spacious home. He was pleased to see that the moving truck with all of their furniture had already arrived, and the movers were busily carrying different pieces inside. As he pulled the car up closer to them, he watched as their living room couch emerged from the trailer, lifted up by two burly men who carried it down a narrow metal ramp.

"Dad, can we get out now?" Greg asked, his voice sounding irritable. The 13-year-old was tired from sitting in the car for hours and wanted to get out and look around. His parents had bought the house after a brief visit to Oak Shade, and all he'd seen were a few photos. He needed to check things out.

"Yes, just be careful to not get in the way of the movers. They're carrying lots of heavy stuff. I don't want you to get hurt."

"Yeah, yeah. Ok, Dad. No problem." Greg immediately disengaged his seatbelt and opened the door at the same time. He was out of the car and racing up to the house within seconds.

Barb sighed and ran a set of fingers through her hair. "Well, at least we know he's still got some energy after that trip. I'm exhausted. So glad we're finally here."

Mikey looked over at his slightly disheveled wife and felt a surge of love in his heart. They'd been married for more than 15 years, and it never ceased to amaze him how much he loved her. While not a true romantic, he was still able to identify the fact that he'd been lucky enough to meet his true soul mate—someone who understood his needs, strengths, and weaknesses. She was the most beautiful, loving woman in the world to him. And even with her makeup gone and her hair slightly mussed, he still wanted her sexually and emotionally.

Reaching out, he gently moved a few strands of hair away from her forehead, leaned over, and kissed her tenderly.

"Yes. We're finally home."

———

Unpacking proved to be a monumental task and one that was most definitely not going to get done in a single day. Mikey took over the strategic game plan and split up the workload so that they could all take over different portions:

Barb unpacked all of the clothes and the more accessible items that weren't buried in boxes …

Greg unpacked his room and then helped unpack the kitchen …

And Mikey unpacked the other rooms while making sure that the furniture was all set up the way it needed to be.

By the time six o'clock rolled around, they were all exhausted, dirty, and ready for showers. They took turns using the one bathroom that Barb was able to clean, picked up some burgers from a nearby fast-food joint, and ate in their new kitchen.

By the time the day was over, everyone was exhausted and ready for bed. Despite the mess around them, the Brennier family slept peacefully amidst the chaos.

# 2

## ONE WEEK LATER

---

Mikey sighed loudly as he pulled his car out of the parking lot at Innovitran. The first week at a new job was never easy, and most of it had been spent trying to figure out where the office supplies were located, how the computer systems worked, and what types of products the company sold. On top of that, each evening was spent trying to finish unpacking the house.

It was exhausting.

Thankfully, Barb had done quite a bit of the heavy lifting throughout the week and had unpacked nearly all of the important boxes. The ones that contained photo albums and other non-essential knick-knacks had been placed up in the attic for another time—perhaps a rainy day.

Outside, the sky grumbled in anger. Mikey looked up at the dark swollen clouds that had gathered in the humid sky. He'd heard on the news that a storm had formed in the Gulf of Mexico and was now making its way toward the coast, preparing to trek across the state. The weatherman was predicting that Oak Shade would be in the storm's path around midnight, so Mikey wanted to be sure to get home where it was safe and dry.

When he pulled into the driveway, he could see an orange glow emanating from the windows downstairs. Definitely a welcoming sight after a long and taxing week.

"Hello. I'm home," he said in a singsong fashion, happy to be with his family.

"Hi, Dad," Greg called from upstairs where he was playing the latest video game of the season.

Mikey knew that Greg would be starting school in a month and quietly hoped that the transition would be an easy one. It was never a simple task to uproot and move a teenager to a new location.

He looked upstairs and considered checking in on his son, but the tantalizing aroma of garlic bread and Spaghetti Carbonara (Barb's specialty) wafted throughout the room. It was too good to ignore, and Mikey found himself moving toward the kitchen as if under a spell.

"That smells amazing," he said, walking into the kitchen and giving Barb a kiss on the top of her head. She was surrounded by steaming pans and bubbling sauces and did not appreciate the interruption.

"Come on, I'm trying to get this special dinner pulled together because it's the end of your first week. I wanted us to celebrate. Stop distracting me."

"Aww come on, I just wanna show you how much I appreciate you." And with that, Mikey grabbed his wife's waist and swung her around, kissing her deeply.

Despite her obvious concentration on the meal preparations, Barb could feel her body responding to Mikey's hardening erection. Despite herself, she moaned softly and pushed herself against him.

"That's so gross. Would you guys please stop it?" a voice whined from behind them.

Mikey laughed and released the hold on his wife, subtly adjusting his slacks so that his obvious and sudden desires weren't apparent.

"So, you decided to leave the video games for a moment? I'm impressed," Mikey joked. "Why don't you help me set the table for dinner?"

---

The pasta was delicious, and Mikey felt the warmth of the meal satisfy the ache in his stomach. For the first time all week, he felt like they were truly *home*. Instead of leading the conversation, he watched his wife and son tease each other and chat about normal, silly things. It made him happy and gave him hope that their lives were heading in the right direction.

Then, suddenly, there was a low grumble of thunder in the distance.

"Sounds like a storm's coming," Barb lamented. "It's the first one since we got here, isn't it?"

"Yeah, Mom," Greg answered. "It's supposed to be a good one. Lots of rain. At least that's what the weather guy was saying on TV this morning."

"You were watching TV this morning?" Mikey asked. "You know the rule. No TV during meals."

His son sighed loudly as if the weight of the world was on his shoulders. "Dad. I only turned it on for a minute because Mom wanted to see if there was traffic on the way to the store. That's all."

The sky grumbled again.

Mikey, not wanting to get into a disagreement and ruin the evening, chose to smile in response.

———————

Later that evening after Greg was asleep, Mikey went into the master bedroom. Barb was in bed, propped up against the pillows, and reading a romance novel.

Outside, the rain had begun, and he could hear the *tap tap tap* sound of tiny drops of water hitting the roof from different angles. The wind had also picked up, and every so often would howl in a low baritone.

Mikey found storms comforting and natural. Having spent so much time in Florida, he was accustomed to evening thunderstorms that lasted for hours and would then become a memory after the hot sun of morning rose over the once-drenched land, quickly drying up any vestiges of rough weather. It was truly amazing to him how storms in the "Sunshine State" could be fleeting yet so ferocious at the same time.

"Hey, babe," he said, sliding under the soft sheets. "Thanks for a great dinner tonight."

Barb smiled at him while she continued reading, but Mikey had other things on his mind. Their mini-makeout session in the kitchen had him thinking about her body and the pleasure she often brought to him.

He moaned softly, stretching out among the soft sheets and felt his body tingle with anticipation. His hands slowly reached out and touched the pale skin of her legs. Then his fingers traveled along her thigh, reaching around the satin of her panties—continually stroking her skin and feeling the slight wetness of her sex.

Barb had now arched her back, and the book she'd been reading fell by the wayside, skidding against the edge of the bed and dropping to the ground with a gentle thud. She turned her head left and then right as Mikey worked his fingers in a manner that he knew would bring her pleasure.

When he felt her body responding, he removed all of Barb's clothes and then his own, subsequently lifting his naked body over hers and beginning their sex dance. It was wonderful and gently hot; building in passion and anticipation.

And when it was over, Mikey laid in bed next to his beloved wife, listening to the rain as it pelted the roof in a continual assault. His eyelids began to grow heavy and ultimately closed as he drifted off to sleep.

---

When Mikey opened his eyes, it was morning and the rain was gone—replaced by strong rays of sunlight that were piercing his eyes like lasers.

He groaned, and through half-slits was able to easily locate the source of his discomfort. The blinds they'd put up over the master bedroom windows were slightly off balance leaving a larger-than-normal gap that the sun had discovered and was proudly manipulating to its advantage.

Pulling the covers over his head, Mikey was about to go back to sleep when a voice downstairs cut through his reverie.

"Dad. Dad!" shouted Greg from somewhere in the house.

Mikey wondered if his son knew the meaning of 'sleeping in'. Most teens took advantage of the weekend in order to catch up on sleep. But his son never did and was always up by six or seven o'clock. Trying to ignore the insistent calling, he grabbed a pillow and wrapped it around his head.

"Dad!"

"Dear God, just go see what he wants," Barb mumbled. She too had wrapped her head in a pillow to try to block out the sound of their son's voice.

"Ok, ok," he grunted.

"Dad!"

"I'm coming," Mikey called out, feeling irritation bubbling up in his mind.

*It's the weekend for Christ's sake.*

First, he ambled into the bathroom for a morning piss, then looked into the mirror. A haggard and tired middle-aged man was all he could see staring back at him. Shaking his head, he quickly splashed water on his face and slowly made his way to the door. On the way, he grabbed a pair of sweatpants and quickly pulled them on, simultaneously sliding his feet into a pair of brown slippers.

"Shut the door behind you," mumbled Barb from the bed.

"Yes, princess," he answered, chuckling at his own joke.

The hallway was bright from a grouping of windows that still remained uncovered and needed blinds. Mikey wondered why they'd decided on a house with so many damned windows but figured that Barb enjoyed the natural lighting. It was the spacious layout and airy feel that had sold them on the house to begin with, so he didn't want to start complaining about it.

"Where are you?" he asked, after ducking his head into Greg's room. It was empty.

"I'm down here, Dad," Greg called out.

Mikey made his way downstairs and saw his son standing in the living room by a set of windows that faced the street. The teen was looking up with concern.

*Oh shit. What the fuck is going on?*

"Dad, check it out," said Greg, who was now pointing at the ceiling. "I was downstairs grabbing some cereal when I heard

15

this dripping noise. I came in here and saw that. We've got a roof leak or something."

Mikey looked up and could see a large wet spot on the ceiling. He too, could hear the dripping, so he pulled away the blinds, and to his dismay could see drops of water hanging at the top of the pane. Every so often, one of the drops would detach and fall to the bottom of the windowsill, hitting the metal grid and splashing against the sofa that was backed up against the wall.

He reached out and touched the back of the sofa. It was damp, which meant that during the rainy night, the water had continuously dripped down, hit the pane, and continued to drench one of his favorite pieces of furniture.

"Crap, let's get some towels and dry this off. Then we'll figure out what to do."

Mikey and Greg grabbed a handful of towels from a nearby closet and began wiping off the windowsill and the couch. Since the sun was beaming through the panes of glass and the air conditioning was blowing on high inside the house, it didn't take them long to dry everything off, but Mikey could tell that water was still caught somewhere because every once in a while, a drop would appear at the top of the window pane.

Taking a deep breath, he tried to keep his temper in check, but Mikey was monumentally pissed off. During the appraisal and inspection of the house, the roof had checked out just fine. Yes, he'd been told that it was nearly 20 years old and would need to be fixed or replaced eventually—but this was bullshit. One major rainstorm, and he was already finding leaks?

Figuring that it might be better to get some fresh air than upset his son, Mikey made a quick decision to take a walk outside and see if any damage had been done to the roof overnight. That way he could calm down and take a look around.

"I'm going to go outside and check the rest of the house, ok?"

Greg nodded.

"Just stay inside and have your breakfast. I'll be right back."

Mikey didn't wait for a response, and instead walked outside, closing the front door behind him. Once on the lawn and away from his son, he took a deep breath and tried to maintain his composure before he lost his mind in total aggravation.

The weather outside was like wading through a bowl of soup. It was extremely humid, and the air was heavy. It still smelled of rain, and the grass was wet underneath his feet. A few clouds hung in the sky, but for the most part it was sunny and incredibly hot.

Mikey looked up at his roof and scanned the perimeter for any obvious signs of damage. The tiles all seemed to be in place, and nothing looked broken. Not unfamiliar with roof repair, he knew that that the problem was underneath the tiles, and that he possibly had a tear in the roof that the inspectors hadn't seen. It would be impossible for him to detect—even if he climbed up on the roof and carefully looked for it.

He knew what this meant.

It would be necessary to hire a roofer.

*Shit.*

"Hey, are you ok? Is your roof alright?"

Surprised to hear someone so close by, Mikey turned around and came face-to-face with someone he'd never seen before.

The man wasn't very tall, but made up for his shorter stature with girth. He was pale with tousled brown hair that was on the verge of appearing greasy. The man's face was as stout as the rest of his body, and his cheeks were red. Two bright blue eyes stared out with concern.

Mikey looked toward the street and saw a white van parked along the curb that read "Renovators Deluxe." A bored-looking passenger sat in the van and hung his arm out of an open window, while he sat facing forward, and seemed to be completely ignoring them both.

"Yes, I'm fine. It's just my roof."

The man chuckled, and when he spoke, Mikey could hear a southern accent that was common in the western parts of Florida.

"Yep. Saw you standing out here on the lawn looking up. Was going to just keep drivin', but figured I'd pull over and see what's happening here. We're on our way to a job, but if you'd like, we can take a quick look and see if we can figure out what's goin' on."

Mikey sighed and stared at his roof in utter frustration. He really didn't want to start dealing with repairs on his first weekend off, but he was going to call a roofer anyway, so he figured it wouldn't hurt to let the guy take a look.

"Sure, thanks. By the way, my name's Mikey."

The stout man smiled and extended a beefy arm. "Nice to meet ya, Mikey. Name's Bob Tansa. I'm one of the owners of "Renovators Deluxe." We specialize in all kinds of house repair. Don't you worry about this. Me and Manuel over there will take a quick look for free and let you know what's goin' on. If you want to hire us to do the work that's fine. If y'all decide on someone else, well that's fine too. There's nothing worse than a leaky roof."

Mikey nodded and started to feel a little better about the situation. Normally, he was used to calling a few companies and giving them the chance to bid on the job, but it was Saturday, it was hot, and hell ... he just wanted someone to fix his problem.

"Sounds good. Thank you."

"No problem at all."

Mikey watched as Bob headed back to the van. The bright sign on the side of the vehicle glinted in the sunlight.

# 3

The thud of someone walking on the roof woke Barb out of a dream that was slowly turning into a nightmare. She'd been eating at a fancy table on board a luxury cruise ship, surrounded by cheerful people, and she had been preparing to dive into a delicious slice of chocolate cake when the loud sounds began.

At first, she tried to ignore the noise and focus on the sweet delight in front of her, but it kept getting louder and louder. And then the thudding started to sound like someone was screaming. It got increasingly shrill when suddenly she heard a voice shout out—

*Then there was fire!*

*Then there was rain!*

*Then there was destruction!*

*You're all going to die! You're all going to die!*

The voice was male and piercing, shooting straight through her skull like an arrow of fire. She jumped up quickly, a shriek emerging from her dry lips. Sitting up in bed, Barb could feel beads of sweat lining her forehead and dripping down her back causing her satin pajama top to stick to her body.

She was shaking, and the memory of the shrieking voice continued to assault her as she tried to remain as still as possible. For a moment, she forgot where she was, and a furtive reach to her right relayed the fact that her husband was not in bed with her. Her only comfort was the sunlight shining through the blinds.

Slowly, the realization that she'd just been in the throes of a nightmare became clear, and every muscle in Barb's body began to relax.

*Ok, no need to freak out. It's just morning, and we're at home, and—wait, what the hell is that noise?*

The thudding began again, and this time, Barb could hear male voices talking. She started to get worried that maybe someone was trying to break in.

*Where the hell is Mikey? Oh shit, I hope he's not trying to fix the roof. He's terrible at repairs.*

Suddenly the bedroom door flew open, and Barb managed to suppress a scream. She was thankful for maintaining control because her son stood in the doorway with an excited look on his face. He held a bowl of cereal in one hand.

"Mom, do you hear the guys on the roof?" he asked quickly. "There's water leaking into our living room, and Dad is outside talking to some guys who fix houses. I think they're on the roof now, checking it out."

Despite feeling relief that her house wasn't being raided by cat burglars, a cold feeling of dread was making its way through her body. The last thing they needed were more expenses given that they'd just spent a fortune on the move. Even though Mikey's new employer had paid for most of the relocation, they'd been spending money on appliances, furniture, and other items for the house. Hooking up all the utilities hadn't been cheap either. And roof repairs were expensive.

Roof replacement was even more damned expensive.

Trying not to sound upset, Barb smiled at Greg and waved him off, "Ok, ok. Let me get out of bed, and then I'll come down and see what's going on."

Greg smiled and ran back down the stairs, balancing the bowl in one hand.

*No doubt to check on what his dad is up to. I'd better do the same. Don't want anybody taking advantage of him.*

Just then, Barb heard one of the men laugh loudly and belch.

*Gross. I'd better hurry up.*

---

Once she'd used the bathroom, washed her face, and brushed her teeth, Barb put on some clothes and headed downstairs. The entire house was bright and sunny, reminding her that life in Oak Shade was a fresh start. She tried to hang on to positive thoughts as she looked to see what was happening in the living room.

There was a large wet spot on the ceiling, but as far as she could tell, water wasn't dripping anywhere. A set of towels had been left in the walkway, and Barb figured that her boys had mopped everything up already. Still, another heavy rain would create even more damage, so something definitely needed to be done quickly.

She looked out the window and saw Mikey standing on the lawn. Remembering the male voices, Barb decided to join him and find out who he was talking to.

At first, she wasn't completely sure what was happening. Mikey was standing in the yard with his hands on his hips, staring up at the roof. As she got closer to him, she spotted the white van parked along the street, with the words "Renovators Deluxe" plastered on the side.

"Honey, I'm glad you're up. Did you see the living room?"

"Yeah, I saw it. Who're these people? Did you call them first thing? They showed up pretty quickly."

Mikey smiled. "They were driving by and saw me standing out here looking at the roof. Pretty lucky that they just happened to be in the neighborhood, huh? Anyway, they came out, and they're checking our roof for free. I'm sure they'll quote me on the job in a few minutes."

"Mikey, can we afford this? I mean, we've got so many expenses."

Mikey seemed frustrated with her response. Barb knew that he felt like she always went straight to the negatives instead of trying to be optimistic. He probably felt that they needed to fix the problem and then move on, whereas she was a bit more practical and liked to consider all angles.

"Look," he said, obviously trying to keep his voice calm. "You know as well as I do that it rains almost every day in Florida during the summer. We're just lucky that it didn't rain earlier this week. We've gotta fix this before it gets worse. Don't you think?"

Barb nodded and decided not to pursue the matter further. It would just cause an argument.

As if on cue, a chubby man came walking up to them. He was accompanied by a colleague who looked like a fellow workman.

"Hi there. I'm Bob. Nice to meet ya."

Bob extended his hand, which Barb accepted hesitantly. He looked dirty and unkempt, but she tried to keep her judgment at bay.

*Don't judge this guy. Give him a chance. So he looks a little greasy. Maybe he's really good at what he does.*

"Nice to meet you too, Bob. So, what do you think is wrong with our roof?"

Bob wiped off his forehead and looked back at Manuel who shook his head and stared at the ground.

"Let me put it this way. Your roof is in rough shape. It's gotta be more than 20 years old. But it's hard to tell from up top what's going on. I'd like to go into your attic, and take a look around. Chances are, you've got holes in the basic roof where the paper's worn down and maybe even large gaps in some places. Can me and Manuel take a look inside, please?"

"Sure," said Mikey. "Let me show you how to get into the attic."

Mikey and the men went into the house and left Barb standing outside in the humidity.

------

Twenty minutes later, the men came downstairs looking sweaty and concerned. Barb had been sitting on the couch while she waited for them, sipping coffee and hoping that the damage wasn't too extensive.

Bob began talking first while Mikey stood nearby and listened intently.

"Well, you've got roof problems, there's no doubt about that. Not sure why it just started now—probably bad luck I guess since y'all just moved here. Last night, the rain leaked in through some spots in the front of your house, traveled down the attic walls and into your living room. There's damp wood in your attic, and it's pretty obvious where the water got in."

"So, what do you suggest?" Mikey asked nervously.

"I think you need to at least repair the spots that are letting water leak in. Eventually, you'll need to replace the entire roof."

Barb cut in, "We're not ready to do that just yet. How much will it cost us to fix the leak?"

Bob chuckled, and it immediately bothered her. The situation wasn't funny, and she didn't appreciate that he found humor in their misfortune.

"Miss, it will probably cost you around two to three thousand dollars. But, you're gonna end up—"

"That sounds fine," she said, interrupting him again. "Why don't you leave your card, and then we'll call you later today to let you know if we need your help."

Mikey looked over at his wife questioningly but figured it would be better to keep quiet than get into an argument in front of the guys from "Renovators Deluxe."

Bob looked back at Manuel, and they both wore expressions like *Ok, it's her choice, but it isn't the right one. And when it rains again, they're both up shit's creek without any semblance of a paddle.* Then he turned to face Barb and Mikey with a smile.

"Alrighty. Hope we can help you folks. Just give us a call when you're ready."

And with that, Bob dropped his card on the table, and the two men left without another word.

———————

"I can't believe you did that. We need to get this fixed. Today." Mikey was aggravated. They'd sent Greg to take a shower so that they could argue in peace.

"It's expensive, Mikey. I figured we'd at least get a quote from one other company."

"Are you kidding me? It's probably going to rain today, and there's no guarantee that another company will come out as quickly. I don't want our new home getting any further damage. Please, just work with me on this."

Barb looked at him and quickly debated her options. She could keep arguing or just give in. And part of her knew that the house and their 'new life' meant the world to Mikey. So instead of continuing the argument, she sighed and looked out the window.

"Fine," she said. "Call them back, and see if they can start immediately. But we are not replacing the damned thing. We're just making a few repairs until we have the money to do a full replacement. Don't let them upsell you."

Mikey smiled and instead of responding, went over and gave his wife a big hug.

He reminded himself—*everything is going to be fine.*

# 4

Greg hummed as he got ready for a shower. One of the benefits of the new house was that he got his own bathroom. It was a highlight because he wasn't thrilled about starting a new school and the fact that all of his friends now lived so far away.

Sure, he could email and text and call, but it wasn't the same as hanging out with his 'boys'.

Pulling off his shirt, he thought about the mess in the living room. In their old home, they'd never had any real issues other than the occasional cockroach or broken appliance. A leaky roof was never a concern because their house had been relatively new and in a newer neighborhood.

Greg was about to turn on the shower when he heard voices outside. His bathroom was upstairs with a window that faced the street, so he carefully pulled back the blinds to see what was going on.

The workmen who'd been talking to his father stood outside the white "Renovators Deluxe" van. He could see that the small fat guy was in front of the vehicle squatting down like he was looking for something. Greg wasn't sure what he was doing, but it seemed weird like perhaps he was checking the transmission.

Suddenly, Bob turned and stared in Greg's direction— almost as if he could tell that someone was watching him.

Greg stepped back, surprised to see the man facing him.

Bob smiled and stuck out his tongue, wiggling it back and forth.

Greg jumped and quickly stepped away from the window.

*There's no way he just did that. What the hell?*

Trembling, Greg went back to the window and looked out fearfully.

The van was gone.

"What?" he asked out loud.

*Maybe I just imagined it, because I didn't even hear the van pull away. How could they have driven off so fast? That is totally weird.*

Greg strained his eyes to see down the street, but other than a kid on a bicycle, there weren't any vehicles passing by from either direction.

Now a little unnerved, he carefully got into the shower and turned on the water, allowing the spray to cover him in a warm blanket.

But even under the familiar comfort of the powerful wet embrace, the vision of the man wiggling his tongue and smiling was stuck in his mind.

And it was making him nauseous.

# 5

The sky grumbled, and Mikey felt his stomach tighten as he rested on the couch watching a movie with Barb. Even though he'd called Bob right back, a woman had answered the phone and told him in a whiny voice that the soonest they could come back out for repairs was Monday.

That meant their house would be vulnerable to the weather all weekend long. And it was looking like it might rain again.

Barb also heard the sound, and looked at Mikey with fear in her eyes. "Do you think we should cover the roof with something?"

"Yeah, I'll go out and get a tarp to put on the roof until Monday."

Rising from the couch, Mikey started to feel a strange sensation that was unfamiliar to him.

He was feeling *spiteful*. And the thoughts that started tumbling through his mind were foreign in their ferocity and direction.

*I've done everything I can to move this family in the right direction. Started a new job, moved us into this beautiful house, put everything behind me—and damn it, I can't even find a few minutes of peace for myself. Why doesn't she go get the fucking tarp?*

Without even thinking about it, Mikey grabbed his keys off the table and stormed out of the living room. He could feel Barb's eyes following him as he walked to the door, threw it open, and slammed it just a bit too hard as he rushed out.

Once behind the wheel of his car, he felt slightly better, and the angry waves that had been washing over him subsided, leaving him with a sense of weariness.

He looked back at his home and sighed. It was a beautiful place and somewhere that anyone would love to live in. One way or the other, they'd make it work.

----

Barb watched as Mikey sped away. She was surprised that he'd suddenly become so angry and figured he was just annoyed that he had to get up and move around instead of simply loafing on the couch, continuing to watch TV.

She turned as Greg's footsteps came echoing down the stairs. He'd been upstairs in his room most of the day and was a bit quieter than usual.

"What's going on, sweetheart?" she asked as he came into the living room, a yogurt in his hand.

"Nothing much. Just kinda hungry. Where's Dad?"

"He went out to get a tarp for the roof because we're expecting more rain later today, and we're not getting it fixed until Monday."

At the mention of roof repairs, Greg's eyes widened. He tried not to look too interested and casually flopped on to the couch.

"So, are you gonna use that company that came out today?"

Barb groaned. "Yes. And it's going to cost us thousands of dollars. But at least they'll come out quickly, and we'll get it fixed.

"Mom?"

"Yes?"

"Don't you think it might be better for us to at least check with some other companies before making a decision? That way, we go for the best deal. I know you said it was gonna be kind of expensive."

Barb leaned over and ruffled her son's soft brown hair. She loved when he was considerate and wondered if maybe he was also worried about their money situation.

"Normally Dad would have checked with some other companies but there's unfortunately not much time. We've got to get this done quickly, and the guys with 'Renovators Deluxe' seemed ok, didn't they?"

Greg didn't answer right away, which surprised her.

"They did seem ok, didn't they?" she repeated.

Greg nodded and tried to push thoughts of the chubby man out of his head, but he could still see him red and sweaty, standing outside with an evil grin on his face as he wiggled his pink tongue with gusto.

---

The rains came, but thankfully, Mikey had enough time to drape a large blue tarp over most of the affected roof, and used a second tarp he'd purchased to cover some of the attic's interior—particularly where the wood was damp as Bob had pointed out. He knew it was a temporary solution, but at least the water wasn't continuing to drip down the wall into the living room.

First it thundered loudly, and then the winds picked up. When the drops started hitting the house, he looked over at his wife and nodded. She smiled back at him, and they silently agreed (reservations or not) that hiring "Renovators Deluxe" was the right decision.

# 6

## *ROOF RENOVATION - DAY ONE*

---

B arb waved at Mikey as he got into his car and drove off. The work week was beginning once more and now she was stuck dealing with the roof repairs, which she knew would be loud and annoying.

The weekend had been a rainy one, and though she'd tried not to watch as the damage was being done, she could see the wet spot on the ceiling in the living room getting larger and darker.

Mikey had checked in the attic numerous times, trying to stem the flow. But somehow the water continued to leak in—even with the tarps in place.

So despite feeling aggravated that she now had to deal with people banging and trespassing on and in her house, the alternative was unthinkable. In fact, the weatherman had been predicting rain throughout the week, so it was probably better to get everything handled now.

She watched as Bob emerged from the van. He was still sweaty, red-faced, and thoroughly unkempt even though it was early in the morning, and she couldn't imagine that he'd had any other jobs yet. This time, another man emerged from the passenger side, and together they went to the back of the truck, pulling out different tools.

There were errands that Barb needed to run, but she knew that it was out of the question to leave if the men were going to be working inside the house for any reason. Mikey had said that there was probably no need, but she should at least ask them before going anywhere.

"Hi," she called out, emerging from the house. "How's it going?"

The men were still behind the van, and she thought she heard one of them mutter, "Dumb bitch."

The words caused her to falter, and she suddenly remembered her nightmare.

*You're all going to die! You're all going to die!*

Trying to calm the sudden rash of nerves that threatened to overtake her, Barb called out again.

"Hi, guys."

This time, Bob came around the van with a large grin on his face.

"Why, hello there! We're just about to get started. Don't worry about us; we'll be sure to stay out of your hair."

Relief flooded through her. "So, you're not going to work inside?"

"No, ma'am. All of this work is done on the outside. You'll hear some hammering and pounding, but other than that—we shouldn't be a bother."

"Ok, great. Well, my son may be at home for a little bit. I'm going to take off."

At the mention of her son, Barb thought she saw Bob's upper lip curl into a sneer, but it was extremely bright outside so she wasn't sure if he was trying to be disrespectful or if it was just a trick of the light.

She decided to give him the benefit of the doubt and let it go.

"No worries. Do what you need to do." And with that, Bob turned away and continued to pull out tools from the back of his van.

It was a normal exchange, and yet Barb couldn't help but feel a bit uneasy. She wasn't sure why something seemed wrong and figured that she'd been hearing things.

*Bob would never call me a bitch, would he?*

*That would be crazy.*

Shaking her head, she turned and went back inside.

Greg was sitting on the couch watching TV, a bathing suit lying on the armrest.

"Greg, you can't sit indoors all day. I know we're still in summer break, but you need to get out a little bit. We already agreed that you were going to ride your bike over to the Community Pool. It's only a few minutes away from here, and it would do you good to get out a little. Don't just sit inside, ok? I don't want to come back and find you still sitting in front of the TV. Understand?"

Greg nodded and kept his eyes on the screen. "Are those guys starting on the roof this morning, Mom?"

Barb looked out the windows that faced the street. She could see Bob carrying a ladder toward the house.

"Yes, they're starting today. So try to stay out of their way, and just do what you need to do."

---

Greg was scared.

He didn't want to stay in the house while the workmen fixed the roof. He wasn't sure exactly what had occurred the other day when he'd been in the bathroom, but the whole thing was weird, and he couldn't seem to get the visual out of his mind.

The last thing he wanted to do was sit inside while the creep was working on the roof, so he decided to move quickly and get dressed for the pool.

Careful to move away from any open windows, he raced upstairs to his bedroom and then locked the door. His heart was pounding as he peeled off his shorts and shirt, pulling up a blue bathing suit as expeditiously as possible.

Once he was done with that, Greg stood for a moment. The small hairs on the back of his neck were standing up, and it felt like someone was watching him. Turning his head slowly, he rested his eyes on the window next to his bed. The blinds were closed, and it was impossible for anyone to see in, but he couldn't shake the feeling that the fat man was on the other side with his face pressed up against the glass.

Even though he was frightened, Greg extended his arm, and in one quick motion, lifted the blinds. Bright sunlight filled his room, and he was relieved that the only thing on the other side of the glass was the familiar image of his neighbor's house.

*Phew.*

Feeling a bit braver now, Greg descended the stairs, grabbed a towel, and left his house. He tried not to turn around, but the sounds of hammering and pounding were too much to ignore. Turning his head, he could see the fat body of Bob Tansa as he hunched over the roof. Bob didn't turn to look at him, and Greg could see sweat dripping off the man's body as he manipulated the hammer in his hand.

Not wanting to be discovered, Greg hopped on his bike and rode away. He didn't realize how fast his heart was beating until he'd ridden all the way to the pool.

It dawned on him that he was happy to be away from his house and the strange men who'd descended upon them.

---

While the house took on blow after blow to its damaged roof, the walls inside shuddered and groaned. And in the corner of the hallway that led from the Master bedroom to Greg's, an air conditioning vent that had been cut into the wall began to vibrate.

At first, it was a low rattle, but then the vibrations grew stronger and stronger until the entire metal grate threatened to break free. And then, when the metal had reached its tension threshold—the vibrating suddenly stopped.

Seconds later, a strange stench began to trickle out of the vents. It wasn't a full-on burst of air, but rather spurts of foul puffs.

Had the Brenniers been home, they would have found it odd that the strange smell was occurring, because the air conditioning wasn't blowing. In fact, it remained still and quiet—the temperature at a comfortable 74 °.

Outside, the men continued to pound and hammer.

---

Barb enjoyed being out of the house. Oak Shade wasn't South Florida, but it did have the quaint charm of a smaller town, and there were quite a few specialty shops carrying unique items that could give their home a bit more character.

Trying to not think about the repairs that were now underway, Barb walked through several stores, picking up different knickknacks, and enjoying the cool bursts of air conditioning in each of the boutiques. Some of the stores smelled delicious with the sweet scent of candles wafting in the air and reminding her of childhood visits to buy Christmas decorations and chocolates.

Barb made it a point to smile at each of the women as she moved past fellow customers. To her disappointment, people weren't all that friendly and only a few smiled back—others just ignored her entirely.

It was tough being newcomers. And everything people said about "small town hospitality" wasn't entirely true. In fact, even their new neighbors hadn't stopped by to say hello or to see how they were doing.

She knew that the hammering and construction on the roof was probably irritating to others in the neighborhood. She hoped that it would all be over soon. Bob had predicted that it would only take a week to fix the roof, but she didn't trust him. There was no reason to dislike the man, yet she couldn't help but feel uncomfortable that he was working on their house.

After walking around for a couple of hours, Barb decided on a few items and then slowly got back into her car. She wasn't thrilled about heading back home, but it was hot outside, and they were spending so much money on the construction that she didn't want to blow a load of cash in the shops.

*Don't want to give Mikey a reason to complain.*

Barb wasn't all that happy. She knew it in her heart and had been trying to come to terms with her emotions for a while. Her marriage to Mikey was ok, though sometimes she felt like his misfortunes and inability to provide a stable life had been the catalyst to their whole life-changing situation.

True, she could work and not rely so much on her husband's income, but she'd made it a point to stay home with Greg when he was a baby and when he was older she had only returned to work part time so that she could pick him up from school on time, do homework with him, and be an active parent.

Now that he was a teenager, however, and didn't need her to take care of him as much, she was feeling a bit lost.

Bottom line, she wasn't as marketable as Mikey and couldn't command a salary like his, so she resigned herself to the fact that her future would largely be tied to his ability to get and keep a good job.

When he'd been laid off from his last job, it had been extremely tough. They'd cut into their savings trying to make ends meet and were contemplating selling their house and moving into an apartment when Innovitran had offered him a job.

They'd argued for days about whether or not to leave South Florida. Barb was a native and didn't want to leave her parents and siblings behind to go move to some out-of-the-way, nowhere town for a job that *might* work out.

Eventually, though, Mikey had won the battle and convinced her that moving to Oak Shade was the right thing to do. And she wasn't in disagreement entirely. It was just the damned roof. The idea that there was something so significantly wrong with the house just days after they'd moved in made her feel wronged somehow.

It was unfair.

As her car maneuvered around the neighborhood, their new home came into view. She didn't see Bob on the roof, but the van was still parked outside, so she figured he was around somewhere.

*I just hope he isn't in my house.*

Shuddering at the thought, Barb stepped on the brake and quickly parked her car. Once she got out, she listened for the telltale sounds of hammering but it was quiet.

*Maybe they're on break?*

Barb pulled out her keys and shoved them in the lock, opening the front door and welcoming the cool blast of air conditioning from inside the house.

Immediately, a strange odor entered her nostrils. The unpleasant smell wasn't particularly strong, yet it was definitely lingering. It smelled moldy and foul—like waterlogged shoes that had been left to rot in the dark.

"Where is that coming from?" she asked aloud, not expecting an answer.

Searching the downstairs wing of the house, Barb was unable to find the scent's origin. Everything looked relatively clean and in place. The area of the living room that had experienced the leakage smelled surprisingly normal. She'd thought for sure that the smell of mold was emanating from the drywall where the water had done its damage.

Greg wasn't home yet, so Barb decided to check upstairs and see if perhaps he had something in his room that was causing the odor. And as she climbed the stairs, the smell increased, confirming her suspicions that the source of the issue was upstairs.

As she stepped up on to the landing, the smell surrounded her, literally wafting around her face and assaulting her nostrils. Wrinkling her nose, Barb continued investigating until a burst of the foul stench hit her directly in the face.

Coughing and backing up, Barb peered at the wall and saw the vent. The metal around the grate looked bent and damaged; the edges worn and scratched.

Stepping away, she decided that even though it was sweltering outside, it would be best to turn off the air conditioning so that the smell wouldn't be propelled further throughout the house. She was about to walk over to the thermostat when the sound of chanting filled her ears.

It was coming from outside, and for a moment reminded her of a movie she'd seen where a group of American Indians had been dancing around a fire, chanting and singing in earnest. Only this singing or chanting (she wasn't sure which) was harsher and at times almost sounded like someone was coughing loudly.

Barb stopped in her tracks and strained to hear.

And then, she heard a goat bleating.

*What the fuck?*

The chanting continued louder and louder while the goat bleated in unison. Barb had no idea what the hell was going on, but it seemed impossible that a goat had somehow made its way onto her roof. Anger coursed through her, and she raced toward the window when the voice from her recent nightmare bellowed impossibly in her mind.

*Then there was fire!*

*Then there was rain!*

*Then there was destruction!*

*You're all going to die!*

# 7

## ROOF RENOVATION - DAY TWO

Mikey awoke before Barb and tried to lay in bed as still as possible so as to not wake her. Even though he'd only been awake a few moments, he could already smell the moldy scent that was permeating the upstairs wing and threatening to creep downstairs.

That was the least of his problems.

The day before, he'd arrived home to find Barb drinking her fourth glass of wine, and Greg holed up in his bedroom playing videogames. When he'd asked Barb what was wrong, she just muttered something about too much stress and motioned to the refrigerator, telling him that he was on his own for the evening.

Then she went straight to bed.

Greg had quickly microwaved a gourmet frozen dinner and taken it up to his room, so Mikey was forced to eat alone. When he went upstairs to check on his son, the teenager seemed *off* somehow—barely answering any questions and just focused on the violent video game he was playing.

Mikey felt like everyone in his family had gone temporarily insane for the evening and resigned himself to a scotch and bad reality television. Sleep had finally overtaken him around midnight, and it took every ounce of energy he had to drag himself to bed.

Now he was awake and almost afraid to talk to Barb. Looking over at his wife, he was amazed at how peaceful she looked. Her eyes were closed, and her chest rose and fell as the sounds of rhythmic breathing continued. He loved his wife when she looked like this, and the ache in his heart was sometimes too much to take.

Still, he had questions. Something had happened, and for some reason she'd chosen to shut him out rather than take the time and energy to share what was going on.

Reaching out, he gently touched her shoulder. When she didn't move, he tried again, and this time Barb shifted and moaned in her sleep.

For a brief moment she seemed happy to see him lying next to her, but then her eyes clouded over.

"Good morning, beautiful. How are you? Feeling better than last night?"

Barb didn't answer and turned on her side, ignoring the questions.

Mikey wasn't going to let her off so easy, and gently grasped her arm, pulling her back so that she was once again facing him.

"What's wrong? You're acting really weird, and last night you didn't say a word. Talk to me."

Barb looked away and seemed uncertain. "I'm not sure I wanna tell you. You're going to think I'm nuts."

Now Mikey was genuinely and seriously concerned.

"Ok, what the hell is going on?"

Barb hesitated for a moment and then propped herself up against a pile of pillows. "Mikey, I think something is wrong with the renovators you hired."

He wasn't sure he'd heard her correctly.

"What? What do you mean?"

Barb looked down and pushed a few strands of hair away from her forehead. She wasn't sure how crazy she sounded and now the tears were falling and she couldn't keep the sobs at bay.

"Honey, what's wrong? Come here."

Mikey embraced her, and worry flooded his mind. He was concerned but didn't want to push too hard. He knew that the move had been hard on everyone. Still, she seemed a bit too dramatic, given the situation.

They remained in an embrace for a few moments, and then Barb pulled away and looked at her husband in a pleading manner. "I'm not sure who those people are, but I heard all sorts of noises yesterday, Mikey. And then I heard a weird voice in the house. And the smell coming from the vent. Did you smell that?"

"Yes," he said gently. "But that has nothing to do with Bob and his guys. We've probably got some mold in the vents that needs to be flushed out. What kind of sounds did you hear?"

Barb described the chanting, and decided to keep the goat sounds to herself. It all seemed nuts anyway. After she'd heard the voice bellowing at her, she'd run out of the house, but to her surprise the van was gone.

There was no one there.

Terrified and worried that she was losing her mind, Barb had decided to drink an entire bottle of wine to numb her senses. Anything was better than remembering the voice from her nightmares.

Now, however, in the bright light of morning, she felt differently and wanted Mikey to know what was going on. She felt certain that he needed to find other people to work on their house who could fix the roof and the obvious mold problem.

"We need someone else, ok?"

Mikey sighed and leaned back against the headboard. "Seriously? They've already started working on the roof, and they can probably help us with the mold too. I don't think changing construction crews at this juncture is the right decision. Maybe you just heard something that was on TV and it seemed like it was coming from outside. Let me go talk to Bob today and see if he can fix the mold too. I'll also tell him to keep it down when he's working outside. Would that help?"

Barb glared at him. Then she got up and stormed into the bathroom without looking back.

Within a minute or so, Mikey heard the shower turn on.

———————

Greg knew he was dreaming, but had a sinking sensation that there was nothing he could do about it.

He was in his house and lying in his bed unable to sleep. Darkness surrounded him with the exception of a blue light glowing from underneath his door.

Something was pulling him toward it. It felt like a magnet was gently guiding him out of the bed and on to his feet.

Greg rose in a fluid motion and glided forward, and it was only when he was facing the door that he realized he hadn't walked.

He'd floated.

His feet were several inches off the ground as he hung in mid-air. It wasn't an unpleasant sensation, so he reached down and grasped the knob, opening the door.

The hallway in front of him was infinite and bathed in the same blue light he'd seen under the door. He squinted, but it wasn't clear exactly where the light was coming from.

Greg willed his body to move forward and felt himself float into the hallway. He continued along the corridor that was narrowly flanked by two walls. Occasionally he would pass a door on either side.

As he floated, he wondered where he would end up, and was about to turn around when he saw a door at the end of the hallway that was open. Bright blue light poured out of the entranceway. Moving faster now, Greg pushed himself forward as fast as the dream would allow.

As the opening came into full view, Greg could see shapes moving around inside it. He was able to make out a figure that turned into his mother. And then the other shape morphed and turned into Bob. Only now, Bob wasn't short and fat.

He was taller, and muscles swelled under a white tank top. Some of the kids at Greg's former school jokingly called it a "wife beater" top, but he didn't like the description. The idea of anyone hurting someone's mother was disturbing.

The muscular version of Bob and his mother turned to face each other. They came together and began a strange waltz around the room. Classical music filled the teenager's head as he watched the eerie dance.

The figures moved around in a circular fashion at a pace that continued to increase until they were a blur, twirling and rotating and twirling and rotating.

Then they stopped, and the music ceased.

They were now standing in the middle of the room. Still locked in position, they stared at each other with wide, dead eyes. Bob pulled one of his arms away from Barb's waist and gently stroked her forehead.

She smiled in response.

Greg's heart started beating faster. He knew something was about to happen, and whatever it was, it wasn't going to be good.

Bob opened his mouth and shrieked impossibly loud with a pitch that rang through Greg's ears like a warning siren.

*You're all going to die!*

*You're all going to die!*

And with that, Bob grabbed Barb's head and twisted it off with one quick yank. Then he turned to face Greg and wiggled his tongue at him.

Greg heard another voice shrieking and realized it was his own. He tried to turn quickly, but the world had grown soupy, and he was moving at a snail's pace. Every second became excruciating as he willed his body to turn and run.

It was too late. The new version of Bob was right behind him now, and he could feel the man's hot fetid breath on his back. A cold arm reached out and grabbed him around the waist, pulling him back.

The sensation was unbearable. It was a torturous, tickling sensation that seemed to burn right through his skin.

Greg felt like he was going to pass out. This was death. He was in unbearable pain—

—until his eyes opened, and he woke up in bed.

The sheets were wet, and to his shame, he realized that for the first time in many years, he'd wet the bed.

---

Mikey couldn't believe how his wife was acting. It was completely irrational and a bit frightening that she believed some guy who owned a renovation company was sitting on their roof, chanting and carrying on.

*Ridiculous.*

*Maybe she's just stressed out about the new house and needs a couple of days away.*

Barb was now refusing to speak to him, and after getting out of the shower, she'd left the house in a huff, peeling out of the driveway.

Greg was still upstairs sleeping, so Mikey was alone downstairs eating a bowl of cold cereal and drinking a cup of coffee that never tasted as good as when his wife made it.

Barb had mentioned that "Renovators Deluxe" usually showed up around nine o'clock, so he decided to text his boss that he was running a few minutes late and waited for Greg to wake up. He was also waiting for Bob to show up so that he could talk to him about the moldy smell coming out of the vent.

Mikey knew that the smell of mold was never a good thing but figured that a good cleaning would take care of the problem since it only seemed to be coming out of that one particular spot. Thankfully, even though it still looked pretty bad, there was no mold growing on or around the wet spot in the living room, and the downstairs smelled fine.

*Thank heavens for little wins along the way, eh?*

He chuckled to himself and went over to the sink to wash out his coffee cup when he saw the now-familiar white van pull up alongside the curb. Mikey was about to go outside and greet the men, when something inside of him advised it might be best to just watch the guys for a moment.

On this particular day, Bob was dressed in a white Miami Dolphins T-shirt, and his shorts were crumpled and stained. He was wearing a worn baseball cap on his head and looked sweaty already.

*Poor guy,* Mikey thought. *Must be tough having to work outside for a living. Hell, I'd be chanting too. Chanting for the damned rain to come pouring down so I'd get some relief.*

Another man stepped out of the van, and it wasn't someone Mikey recognized. He found it odd that Bob was always bringing different people with him to work on the house. It seemed like "Renovators Deluxe" was a small operation, but Bob's staff seemed immense. Whenever Mikey saw them leave for the day, Bob was always accompanied by a new person.

In fact, Mikey realized that other than Bob, he'd never seen the same face twice.

*Weird.*

Bob and the man were pulling tools out of the rear of the van when Mikey saw something strange. The men were standing next to each other, and the tops of their bodies were obscured by the open doors of the van. He could see their waists and legs, but then he saw something else too.

As some of the tools came tumbling out, a darker reddish object emerged and was now hanging over the edge of the van.

Mikey squinted to see what it was and could barely make it out. It looked like a strap or a whip.

Just then, Bob turned and looked in his direction.

Mikey stepped away from the window and tried to breathe. His heart was pounding, and he felt like a weirdo, spying on the workmen. Taking a deep breath, he walked out of the kitchen and went outside. As he got closer to the van, he could hear Bob giving the other man specific instructions on what had to be done to the roof.

"And be sure you move around carefully," he was saying. "Some of those tiles are mighty fragile, don't you think?"

Then the two men laughed.

Mikey wasn't sure what was so funny, but figured it was an inside joke. He walked over to the men and cleared his throat to ensure they knew that he'd arrived.

Bob gave him a large smile. "Hey, there! How're you? We're right on schedule. Should be done with yer roof sometime in the next few days."

Mikey couldn't help himself. "What's that?" he asked, pointing to the strange object which, up close, looked like a medieval whip.

Bob laughed heartily. "Aw, that thing? I should've put that away. Quite sorry. It's something I use with the missus once in a while. We've been married for what seems like an eternity, so sometimes we have to liven things up, you know?"

And then the man licked his lips as if to stress the point.

The idea was grotesque, and Mikey felt sick, so he decided to change the subject. "Listen, we have some sort of mold problem now, too. We're smelling a strange odor upstairs out of one of the vents, and we think it might be a problem inside the duct somewhere."

At the mention of mold, Bob crinkled up his forehead and sighed. "I ain't surprised. These houses are old, and with all the rain we get around here and the problems with yer roof, well, it's just a disaster waiting to happen. The good news is, we can handle it for you, but I'm gonna need to take a look around on the inside of your house. Mind if we come in for a minute?"

Mikey nodded, and at the same time a small voice in his mind screamed *No! This is your sacred place. Don't let him in. He's dirty and there's that whip. What is he really using it for?*

Mikey tried to ignore his inner alarm, and instead led Bob and the other man (who hadn't been introduced) inside his home. As the men passed him on the way in, he could smell their unwashed bodies and wondered why the men chose to not wear deodorant.

As they walked through, Bob craned his neck and looked at the different rooms. "Nice place you have here. It looks nicer every time I come inside."

Mikey led the men up the stairs to the attic entrance, which was inconveniently located inside of Barb's walk-in closet. He didn't like having the men traipsing through the house, but there was really no other way to get them to the attic.

"Where's your boy?" Bob asked with a grin. "He running around already with the kids in the neighborhood?"

Mikey chose to ignore the question, and instead, reached up and pulled on a long string that brought down the entire trapdoor and makeshift ladder. "Ok, here you go."

---

The men moved around the attic for about fifteen minutes and then slowly emerged. Bob shook his head and wiped sweat off his red forehead. "We've gotta do some serious work to your air ducts. There's a hole in one of your ducts, and I think water's gotten in there and started your mold problem. We can work on this right now if you want, and I'll just split my crews so you're not stuck. Whaddaya say?"

Mikey didn't know what to say. He was becoming increasingly distraught with the problems the house was experiencing. He couldn't understand how the inspector had missed all of these things when they'd considered buying it in the first place.

But Bob was waiting for a response, and it was all too overwhelming.

"Ok, just take care of it."

---

Barb was just starting to calm down as she once again turned the corner and headed down the street back to the house. She knew her request that they find new contractors sounded crazy, but Mikey never believed her. He just dismissed her comments as lunacy and assumed that she was having a difficult time handling the move.

And yes, she was stressed out about moving to a new town. Who wouldn't be? Perhaps she'd heard voices that weren't there.

Shaking her head and trying to focus on remaining rational, she ignored the "Renovators Deluxe" van and pulled into the driveway. To her surprise, Mikey's car was still parked near the house, and she could see him talking to someone as he exited with his briefcase in hand.

"What are you still doing here?" she asked, confused.

"Sorry, I'm running really late. Bob got here, and I wanted to tell him about the mold problem. He's going to keep working on the roof while one of his guys works in the attic."

Barb glared at him. Not only were they not going to replace the renovators, but now they were giving these creeps even more work? And having them work in the house on top of it?

*Wonderful. Simply fucking wonderful.*

"I can't believe you. You didn't even ask me what I thought."

Mikey's eyes narrowed into slits. "Oh, really? Well, it was hard to get your opinion when you basically didn't speak to me at all last night, and this morning you left in a hurry. You didn't even take your cell phone with you, so how would I have contacted you? Anyway, Greg's still sleeping, and I'm going to work. I'll check in later."

With that, he turned on his heel and left her standing there.

Barb watched Mikey get into his car and then pull out of the driveway and head down the street. She was so angry and confused that she couldn't even muster up tears or shout at the sky in frustration.

Suddenly, hammering caught her attention, and she looked up at the roof and saw that Bob was hard at work along with another man. She found it strange that there were three men on site today given that Bob usually only traveled with one other person.

*Didn't Mikey say that there was someone inside working on the house?*

Barb thought about calling him and asking whether or not he'd seen additional guys drive up, but given the way he'd left, she decided it would be better to keep her distance for now. There were feelings surging through her that were uncomfortable and serious.

*Not feeling good about my marriage right now or the direction of my life. It might be better to take things one day at a time for now and determine how I'm going to handle all of this once we get the house back in working order.*

It amazed and angered her that they were dealing with so many problems given that they'd just moved into the house. Barb knew that it wasn't supposed to be this way.

Something wasn't right.

Instead of saying hello to the men on the roof, she simply went inside and shut the door.

---

As soon as he heard his father leave the house, Greg rushed to the laundry room with his soiled sheets. He'd been waiting for creepy Bob and his henchman to leave so that he could hide the evidence and spare himself the humiliation of having to explain to his mother why he'd wet the bed.

Greg stuffed his sheets at the bottom of the washing machine and piled other dirty clothes on top. Then he poured detergent inside and started the machine. Once the telltale hum of the appliance began, he went out to the hallway and quickly grabbed a clean sheet. He was about to take it to his room when he heard his mother downstairs.

She was talking to herself, which was something she did when things weren't going well. He could hear her grumbling and sighing, so there wasn't much time to spare.

With all the energy he had pumping through his veins, Greg quickly changed his sheets and made up his bed. He was pulling a bathing suit out of his dresser when he heard his mother approach.

"Hey," she said, sitting down on the bed with an annoyed look on her face. "I think it's probably best if you head to the community center for the day after you eat something for breakfast. These guys are going to be working in the house, and I'd prefer that you stay out of their way. It's gonna be loud and messy."

Greg didn't have to be told twice. There was no way he was going to stay in the house with those strange people working on it. And the mold smell was kind of gross, so he preferred to be out in the fresh air with other kids from the neighborhood. He'd already met some teens who lived a couple of streets over, and they seemed nice enough. So hanging out with them for the day was an appealing option.

"Ok, Mom. I'll grab a towel and head out."

He tried to leave the room without having to stretch out the conversation further, but his mother was extremely observant and gave his bed a hard stare. When she looked back up at him, there was a small smile on her face.

"Did you actually make your own bed? I am *impressed*. Usually that requires some begging and lots of threats," she laughed.

Greg just smiled and hugged his mother. Despite the typical teenage angst that he was starting to deal with, he loved his mother with all of his heart, and liked the way she looked at the world sometimes.

"I love you, Mom."

---

After their tender moment in his bedroom, Greg left his mother upstairs and went into the kitchen to make some toast and jam. He ate quickly and then headed out the front door. He was feeling better about things and figured that his mess was a one-time deal or some sort of fluke. After all, he hadn't wet the bed in years, so there was no reason why it would start up again now.

*I must've had too much to drink before I laid down. Not doing that again.*

"Hey there, young man," a voice called from above.

Greg looked up and saw Bob crouched next to a black patch on the roof. The man was sweaty and red as usual and even looking at him made Greg's skin crawl. To his surprise there was another man on the roof, as well.

*Wonderful. More creepy guys to deal with.*

Trying to mask his uneasiness, the teenager smiled and pointed to his bike. "I'm heading out. Hope you guys get a lot done today."

Bob chuckled, and Greg didn't like it at all. It was an evil sound that was completely out of place.

"Well, you have a good time out there. Always love the feeling of cool water on a hot day. Better than a wet bed in the morning, ain't it?"

Greg's mouth fell open, and for a moment all he could do was stare in shock at the man's red-faced grin.

"Well, what do you prefer? Best to be wet in the pool, ain't it?"

Without answering the awful question, Greg turned and ran to his bike. He could hear Bob laughing loudly, and it seemed as if each bellowed burst was erupting in his head.

He jumped on his bike and pedaled away quickly, but Bob's laughter followed him as he pushed forward down the street, and it was only when the pool came into view that he was able to catch his breath.

---

Mikey stared at his computer screen in dismay. Even though he'd gotten ample sleep the night before, his head felt hazy, and all the words on the screen were running together in a blur. His head also hurt, and he wasn't sure why.

Things were not going as planned, and the situation with their house was slowly unraveling. Feeling a surge of anger, he fished out their realtor's phone number that was still lodged in his wallet. He quickly punched in the digits and waited for the woman to answer, tension building in his shoulders.

The realtor, named Janice, answered on the third ring.

"Hi, this is Janice speaking," she said pleasantly, though Mikey detected a twinge of fatigue.

"Janice, this is Mikey Brennier. I need to talk to you about our house."

The woman paused for a moment and then responded calmly, keeping the positive tone in her voice. "Why yes, hello, Mr. Brennier. It's been a few weeks since we've spoken, and I've been meaning to call you about the new place. How's it going?"

Mikey took a deep breath and tried to maintain his composure. "Well, things aren't exactly going as planned."

He shared with her the issue with the leaky roof and described the moldy smell in great detail. Janice had actually recommended the inspector they used, so he hoped that maybe she could shed some light on why none of the issues were detected upon inspection.

"Mr. Brennier, I'm not sure what to say. When you had the house inspected, everything checked out. It's possible that the damage and the mold happened after the sale, isn't it?"

"With all due respect, Janice, I don't think that's really possible. There must've been issues that the inspector missed. Is there anything I can do about this?"

There was silence on the phone for a moment, and then Janice quietly asked, "Have you hired anyone to help you fix the problems?"

"Yes," Mikey said, his irritation threatening to bubble over. "I hired some guys with a company called 'Renovators Deluxe.' They seem ok, but we just keep finding issues."

He waited for the realtor to respond, but silence greeted him on the other end. After a few uncomfortable seconds, he spoke up. "Hello? Janice, are you there?"

"Um, yeah. Listen, Mr. Brennier, I've got to go take care of something. I'll call you back, ok?"

"Ok," he managed to say before she hung up the phone.

*That was weird. Why did she hang up so fast? Maybe I made her nervous. Well, that's too damned bad. She needs to help me fix this situation. My family can't live in a house that's falling apart. If things keep going wrong, I might even sue the bastards who sold us that damned place to begin with.*

The phone suddenly rang again. Mikey looked down at the display, and to his surprise, the number didn't register on the screen.

He picked up the line, fully expecting to hear a telemarketer on the other line.

"Hello?"

Silence flooded the receiver.

"Hello?" he repeated again.

*Click.*

The phone went dead in his hand.

*That's weird. Maybe it's just a wrong number or something.*

Trying to push the ominous thoughts out of his head, Mikey rubbed his eyes and once again peered at the screen, hoping that the words would make enough sense for him to get on with work and make it through the day.

———————————

Even with the workman moving around in the attic, Barb felt the emptiness of the house surround her. Their new home was considerably larger than the one they'd lived in when they resided in Miami, and she sometimes wondered if they needed all the extra space.

She could still smell the mold, but it was more muted in her bedroom where the gentle scent of lavender permeated the air. She'd been sure to lightly scent her undergarments and linens because the smell always made her feel more relaxed and ethereal. In truth, her bedroom was her sanctuary—a place where she sometimes felt like a spring maiden rejuvenating for the next day.

Looking in the mirror, Barb laughed.

*Some maiden. I look like I've seen better days.*

The reflection that stared back at her wasn't exactly unattractive, per se. It was just a face that had seen many years of change and disappointment. Her once smooth countenance was now lined with a small network of wrinkles and crow's feet that etched themselves into the level areas of her face. Straight brown hair that fell around a spherical frame now contained slivers of shiny gray that peeked through the dark cover of lustrous strands.

Barb knew that she was still good-looking for a nearly middle-aged woman. But sometimes she forgot her own femininity with all that had to be done every day. Somehow, in the midst of folding laundry, making breakfast, lunch or dinner or mopping the floors, those days of feeling like a beautiful princess were lost amidst the mundane tasks of life.

Mikey wasn't necessarily helping in that area, either. While there was no doubt that he was still sexually attracted to her and enjoyed making love (he was a man after all), rarely did he take her with the passion that she yearned for and watched unfold in romance films. And she couldn't remember the last time he'd brought home flowers, perfume, or chocolates. Most of the time, he was wrapped up in his work or the necessities of the day and basically forgot that there were other things that needed to be 'tended to' in order for his significant other to feel … well, *significant*.

A shuffling sound from behind her caused Barb to drop the towel she was folding and turn around quickly. She was surprised to see that the man who'd been up in the attic was slowly making his way down the miniature ladder, and once he got to the ground, he began wiping his hands with a soiled cloth.

She watched him clean his hands off, and despite feeling a bit of fear that there was a virtual stranger standing in her bedroom with no one around to protect her in the event that something went awry, she was shocked to find herself intrigued as well.

He was a tall man and quite attractive. His hair was dark and tousled, as if he'd just gotten out of bed. The man's face was chiseled like a model's—with sharp cheekbones, a small nose, and large velvet lips. His eyes were black as night and seemed to be gazing right through her.

Barb began feeling sensations that had eluded her for a very long time. She could feel her desire build with the increase of her heart rate and then travel through her blood as bursts of adrenaline, only to descend down to her femininity in waves of heat that moistened her private shroud of desire.

*Oh my God. He's so hot. I just want to take him and rub myself all over his sex. What the hell is happening to me?*

The man smiled and said in broken English, "I'm done for a minute. Will be back in a short time. Is that okay, miss?"

Barb caught a whiff of terrible body odor, and for a moment felt her attraction to the strange man wane considerably, but as he drew closer she could see muscles bulging underneath a stained white tank top, and her body began to respond again.

Without even realizing it, her body began to move on its own and brought her closer to the workman. She was now standing right in front of him and didn't even mind the stench that seemed to emit from his every pore. His overwhelming masculinity seethed out in fumes of desire and lust, pulling her closer and closer until she felt as if she would die if she didn't touch him.

The man reached out and touched her face, his skin cold and clammy at first, and then feeling as if it was searing right through her skin.

Barb brought her body closer to his, the aching within her so unbearable that she thought she might melt into a mound of lust.

He smiled, all white gleaming teeth, and then brought his mouth closer, kissing her delicately on the lips.

She moaned and moved her body closer to his, pushing her pelvis against his firm body and feeling his maleness thicken and harden against the tight fabric of his jeans. Without even realizing that she was behaving in such a wanton manner, she rubbed herself against him, thrusting her body back and forth against his pants. She felt herself orgasm impossibly powerfully and then stepped back as her muscles tensed and released small amounts of moisture inside her underwear.

The man smiled and whispered in her ear, "Then there was fire."

His accent was strong, and Barb found it incredibly sexy. Then he walked out of the room and left her standing in place. She swayed for a moment and then crumpled to the ground as a strange exhaustion filled her body and blocked out all thought.

———

The hot Florida summer sun lost its battle against the cool chlorinated waves in the large community pool. The 50-meter pool was Olympic-sized, but instead of hosting an array of swimmers, had become a place of fun and mirth for the heaps of hyperactive children who enjoyed splashing around like miniature guppies.

The water was bright blue and generally helped to elicit a sense of relaxation and enjoyment. But Greg didn't notice anything refreshing about the pool as he rested against the wall with his head propped up on the warm tiles that lined the ground.

His thoughts continued going back to the strange men working on his house. How had Bob known about his bed wetting incident? Surely he hadn't seen anything through the windows because the blinds were closed, and it wasn't something that happened every day.

So, how had the man known about it?

*Maybe he's not a man. Maybe he's something evil.*

Even though it was more than 90° outside, Greg shivered in the water. He wasn't normally a superstitious sort of person, but he had serious doubts about the guys at "Renovators Deluxe."

First of all, as soon as they'd started working on the house, things had been going wrong. The roof wasn't totally fixed yet, and now there was this gross mold problem. His parents were acting weird, and his mother had started drinking, which wasn't something she did often.

Greg wasn't sure whether or not they were in danger and didn't want to overreact. Still, things hadn't been the same since Bob and his colleagues had started on the house, and neither his mother nor his father seemed to notice. In fact, they were just going on like everything was fine.

*Maybe it's up to me to protect them.*

The thought popped into Greg's head like a shooting pain and caused him to stand upright and look around.

*I shouldn't be hanging around here in the pool. I need to be home.*

Without even casting a glance around him or saying goodbye to his new friends, Greg pulled himself out of the pool, dried off quickly, and got on his bike.

He rode home in silence, carefully ensuring that he was following all traffic rules but not allowing his mind to wander in any direction other than the task at hand. His eyes were firmly focused on the road in front of him, and with the exception of the natural need to blink, Greg seemed as stoic as a storefront mannequin.

When he pulled his bike up to the front of the house, he was surprised to now see several men on the roof. The men looked muscled, sweaty, and unfriendly. And Bob was not up there with them. He wondered how many people were inside the house working on the ducts.

Fear shot through his skull, and he quickly laid his bike down on the grass and strode to the front door. He was prepared to call out to his mother, when he found her sitting in the kitchen, a cup of steaming coffee in her hand.

"Mom, how's it going?" he asked.

She didn't answer him immediately, and instead stared out of the window with a faraway look on her face. Greg noticed that her cheeks were rosy, and she seemed very content.

"Mom?"

Barb glanced away from the window and looked at him calmly. She still seemed hazy, and her eyes were moist and distant.

"Mhmm? What're you doing home so early? I thought you were going to be at the pool all day."

Her questions made him feel a bit defensive. Here he'd been rushing home to help her—to protect her—and she was acting like she could care less about whether or not he was around.

"Yeah," he answered, trying to seem nonchalant. "It was just getting too hot out there, so I figured that I would come home and have lunch with you. Is that ok?"

Barb turned away and stared out the window once more. "Sure. I don't have anything though. You wanna take a ride out to Jack's Sub Shop? There's money in my wallet."

Greg was taken aback. His mother *always* made him lunch. What the hell was going on? What was wrong with her?

He was about to protest, but stopped when his mother walked over to the sink and poured an entire cup of coffee down the drain.

"I'm going to take a nap upstairs," she said, and left the room.

Greg tried to shake off the feelings of anxiety that were threatening him, and instead, decided to open the refrigerator and look for something to eat. He was able to find some cheese and lathered up a few slices with mayonnaise, blanketing them with two pieces of white bread.

He stood at the sink, eating his sandwich quickly, concerned thoughts rolling over in his mind.

*What should I do? Should I follow her? Why is she acting this way? Maybe I need to call Dad and have him come home and help me. I was silly to think I can protect this family by myself. I'm only a freaking teenager! This isn't cool.*

Greg swallowed the rest of the sandwich and threw the paper plate he'd been using into the trash. Turning to leave, he found himself face-to-face with a man who had large muscles and piercing eyes. The man smelled awful and looked menacing.

"Escuse me," he said, his accent strong and aggressive. "I go back upstairs to work on ducts."

And with that, he brushed past Greg and headed into the living room. Greg smelled unwashed body odor follow the man as he climbed the stairwell.

Something inside his mind was screaming for him to follow the man and stop whatever might be happening. He took a step forward and then heard strange moaning and bleating sounds coming from the direction of his parent's bedroom.

*It sounds like a goat shrieking in pain.*

Terrified now, Greg decided to stay downstairs and put on his headphones. He sat in front of the television in a nearly catatonic state.

---

Mikey couldn't get out of the office fast enough. All day he'd had a strange suspicion that something wasn't right. After his phone conversation with Janice, he felt like there was something she was hiding from him. And when he'd tried to call her again, the phone rang and rang until her voicemail picked up.

He left a message but hadn't heard back yet.

To make matters worse, as expected, the company was preparing for the launch of brand new product lines, and the workload had increased exponentially. His boss sent an email with a list of things that needed to get done within the month. Mikey was a smart guy, but he was still getting his feet wet and didn't feel completely comfortable jumping in and completing projects that would lay the foundation for the strategy that the company would be taking.

So when five o'clock rolled around, he decided it was time to go. Normally, he was expected to stick around until at least five-thirty, but there was no way he could give any more to the tasks at hand.

After a cursory look down the hallway, Mikey quickly packed up his stuff and briskly walked to his car. Once inside, he dialed the house and was surprised when Barb didn't answer. Normally, she was pleased to have him home on time because that meant they could spend some quality time together.

Mikey smiled to himself. Barb's idea of quality time was sitting on the couch watching some lame sitcom while they snacked on popcorn or M&Ms. He was amazed at how she appreciated the little things in life, though he sometimes wondered if she missed the passions they'd once experienced together in the early years when they could barely keep their hands off of each other.

He was still very attracted to his wife, but somehow the frequency of their lovemaking had waned considerably. In the early days, they'd made love almost every day and sometimes more than once a day. Now, they were lucky if they were able to find the time to have sex once or twice a week. And even though he wanted to blame it on the fact that they had a child and responsibilities, he knew better.

It was very possible that he simply wasn't trying hard enough. He knew that Barb needed romance and flowers and all sorts of stuff that those damned romance novels and movies dictated was the norm. But the reality was—it really wasn't how things went. People had to work every day, and it wasn't as easy as it looked to be romantic all the time. There were other ways to demonstrate love other than a bouquet of roses, jewelry, or a new bottle of perfume.

Still, Mikey thought it might be nice to surprise his wife with an unusual romantic gesture, so he stopped over at the local drugstore on his way home and picked up a box of her favorite brand of chocolate covered cherries. Then he went over to the card aisle and picked out a card that wasn't too mushy and yet was still able to clearly demonstrate his love.

Feeling good about himself now, Mikey gathered up his loot and headed home. As his car pulled around the corner, he was slightly disappointed to see that the roof was still under construction. He wasn't fully sure, but it seemed to look better than it had in the morning. Still, there was a bit of work left to do on it, and he knew that there was more rain on the way.

At least the van wasn't parked in the driveway, which meant that the men with "Renovators Deluxe" were done for the day, and his family was able to get a little private time. He'd calculated the expenses, and he was already looking at close to six thousand dollars in order to get all of the work done.

To make matters worse, he was still waiting on his first paycheck, so they'd be dipping into their savings to pay for the repairs. Still, it needed to be done. They couldn't live in a house with water dripping down the walls and mold growing in the air ducts.

Parking his car in the driveway, Mikey gathered up his gifts for Barb and walked to the front door, whistling as he briskly tread on the soft lawn. He felt better for some reason and was ready for a nice evening together.

When he opened the door, he was surprised to smell the delicious aroma of garlic wafting through the air. The house was brightly lit with Italian opera music wailing out of the portable radio that was resting on the windowsill in the kitchen. From his vantage point, he could see Barb happily cooking a large meal, her face flushed and exuberant.

At first, Mikey wasn't exactly sure how to react. It had been a while since he'd seen his wife so giddy and carefree, but he didn't want to ruin it, so he stepped carefully into the kitchen clutching the box of chocolates and the card.

"Baby!" Barb exclaimed, as she twirled towards him, nearly collapsing into his arms. "How was your day?"

She saw the chocolates and card and shrieked like a schoolgirl. "Thank you so much, darling! That is so nice of you. What a great hubby I have!"

Mikey was taken aback at her overabundance of excitement. He didn't want to seem unappreciative but the woman was acting like she was high on speed. And even though she looked very attractive, there was a scent coming from her skin that wasn't altogether pleasant.

In fact, it was entirely unfamiliar as Barb normally took very good care of herself and bathed regularly. But now, she smelled *unwashed*—like she'd decided to forgo deodorant for the day. The odor caught Mikey off-guard, but he tried to ignore it and focus on how happy she was. And he figured that they could take a bath together later on.

He watched Barb literally do a pirouette back to the oven and continue to mix the sauces she'd prepared. As she worked, he noticed something else a little strange. She was wearing a sundress with a lower than usual cut back that normally revealed smooth skin. This time however, there were little red marks in various places along her shoulders.

They looked like bite marks.

Concerned now, Mikey drew closer to his wife, trying to ignore the body odor that she emitted. "Honey, what's that on your back?"

Barb absentmindedly reached out with a free hand and did a cursory feel, her hand barely grazing the red welts that were along her shoulders and back.

"Oh, that's probably because I was outside pulling some weeds out of the ground. There's so many strange bugs and mosquitoes out there. I'm sure one of them just went to town on me."

She returned to the sauces and started humming a tune as she stirred.

Mikey found her behavior incredibly strange. Usually Barb was a bit of a hypochondriac and worried about every little ache or pain. But now she had these red spots all over her back, and she was acting like everything was just fine.

Pushing his concerns away, Mikey focused on setting the table and tried to ignore his wife's odd behavior.

---

The bizarre behavior continued into their dinner.

For starters, Greg came to the table and barely said a word. Instead, he stared at his plate and pushed the pasta around, making strange shapes. He answered Mikey's questions with a curt grunt and wouldn't look at Barb at all.

As for Barb, she cheerfully sat at the table and bustled about as if everything was fine. Once in a while, Mikey caught a whiff of her unwashed body odor, and it curbed his appetite. So even though the food looked tantalizing, his stomach was tense, and it was hard to eat even half of his portion.

Barb chatted on and on about how things were going to be so great in their new town and seemed to have completely changed her mind about Bob and the other men with "Renovators Deluxe." In fact, she was discussing how happy she was that they were fixing the mold problem.

Mikey was distracted with his own thoughts and tuned her out for the most of the meal. When he finally started paying attention, he realized that he hadn't missed much.

"It is so important," she was saying. "Mold in Florida can be a really bad thing. Friends of mine back home in West Miami where I was growing up had mold in their attic, and they ended up having to tear down the whole house and start over. It can really make you sick and certainly doesn't help you throw great dinner parties!" She laughed—her mouth full of pasta.

Greg looked disgusted and pushed his plate away. "Can I please be excused?" he asked, already beginning to rise from the chair.

Mikey was annoyed. His son had been behaving badly all throughout dinner and was now disrespecting family time by leaving the table and no doubt going to play video games.

"No, young man. I think you need to stay at the table a bit longer. You barely ate any of your dinner."

Barb laughed suddenly and waved her arms dismissively as if to swipe away a gnat. "That's fine. Let him go. He's been quiet all day. He's just a teenager. They're all too cool for their parents, isn't that right, Greg?"

The teenager looked at her miserably and nodded his head quickly—nearly knocking down his chair as he raced out of the kitchen.

"What was that about?" Mikey asked, concern in his voice. He'd never quite seen Greg act in such a nervous manner around them. Usually he was congenial to some degree and being an only child was used to sitting and chatting with his parents.

But Barb had already moved on and was noisily eating a roll while alternatively drinking a glass of wine. Little red droplets dotted the white tablecloth as she commenced her eating and drinking without a care in the world.

---

Greg raced up the stairs as fast as his legs would allow. The upstairs wing still smelled of mold but was a little less intense than it had been earlier in the day. Only now it smelled differently. There was an odor slinking about that smelled like unwashed bodies.

Shaking his head and coughing, he went into his bedroom and locked the door.

Thoughts of what he had seen earlier in the day clouded his mind and sickened him further—

*After his mother and then the strange man had gone upstairs, there had been loud sounds coming from the master bedroom—audible even with his headphones on. At first it sounded like chanting or a demented choir, but then he'd also heard some kind of animal bleating and shrieking. The ceiling started thumping, and all the light fixtures began swaying.*

*Fearful for his safety, Greg decided he had two choices: call his dad or try to handle the situation himself. After careful consideration, he decided it wasn't worth freaking out his father who was working so hard to make their life better in Oak Shade. Even as a self-involved teenager, Greg knew that his dad was putting in everything he had to give him and his mom a better life.*

*Plus, he was nearly a man now anyway, so it was time to step up and handle it on his own.*

*Or at last that's what he tried to tell himself.*

*So he waited a moment or two and then went up the stairs slowly and cautiously.*

*When he reached the landing, he looked in the direction of where the noises were coming from. The hallway leading to his parent's room was dark but strangely enough, the door to their bedroom wasn't completely shut.*

*Greg remembered his nightmare, and fear gripped his heart like a vice. Still, he couldn't help but approach the room, driven by the primal instinct to protect his mother from whatever danger she was in.*

*He could hear shrieks, moans, and thumps and tried to ignore them as he pressed forward. He peered into the doorway, his eyes widening at what was taking place in front of him.*

*His mother was completely naked and straddling a man on the bed. Only it wasn't a man, because it looked like some sort of hybrid-animal resembling a mixture of insect and goat. At first, Greg thought it might just be a person wearing a mask, but when the thing lifted its head and roared with passion and urgency, it was clear that the head was indeed connected to the rest of the body.*

*They rocked together while Greg watched, revulsion filling every thought, every feeling.*

*He shifted, and the ground creaked under his feet. Terrified that his mother and her animal-lover would see him, he turned and raced downstairs, heading straight for the front door. But just as he reached for the knob something stopped him.*

*He couldn't leave his mother in there with that … that creature. He couldn't save her or protect her, so he had no choice but to wait it out. He needed to be around when she was done to make sure that nothing else happened.*

*It seemed like his mother and the creature had sex for hours. But eventually, the "Renovators Deluxe" workman descended the stairwell and left the house.*

*Just before he did, he turned and looked at Greg.*

*The man's face had returned to normal, but his eyes were dark and evil, sending chills through Greg's body. Greg forced himself to maintain a stare and not look away.*

*The workman smiled and winked—then turned and left.*

*As soon as he was alone, Greg raced upstairs to check on his mother. He knew that he might find her naked, but it didn't matter. He had to be sure she was alright.*

*The door to the master bedroom was now fully open and Greg could smell the unwashed body odor pouring out of the room in a fetid mass of invisible smoke. Taking a deep breath, he stepped into the room and was relieved to see that his mother was lying on the bed and wearing her clothes.*

*She was flat on her back, her face upright in such a manner that if she'd actually had her eyes open, she'd be staring straight at the ceiling. Thankfully though, her eyes were peacefully closed, and her chest rose and fell in rhythmic breathing.*

*Greg walked up to the bed and tried to wake her up, but her breath was bad, her clothes were mussed and stank like unwashed body odor, and she seemed to be asleep, so he decided to leave her alone and go play video games in his bedroom.*

*It felt strange trying to destroy techno-enemies when it felt like there was a larger threat living within the walls of their new home. His mother had somehow been sexually attacked by a strange, nameless enemy, and Greg had never felt so helpless.*

*Who could he tell? His father would never believe him, and his new friends would quickly unfriend him, thinking that he was nuts and delusional. He hadn't been smart enough to grab his smartphone and take a photo of the creature that was humping his mother. So he was essentially screwed.*

*When his father had come home, Greg had wanted so badly to tell him what was going on. But something wouldn't allow him to move. He felt molded into the cushions of the couch while his mother, now awake from her strange slumber, bustled about happily as if nothing had ever happened.*

*It was insane.*

And now, sitting in his room by himself, door locked and blinds closed, Greg wondered if perhaps he was losing his mind. Was it possible to start going crazy at the onset of puberty? Maybe there was something in the vitamins he was taking?

*No. I know what I saw. She was having sex with something that couldn't possibly be real.*

It was too much for the teenager to take. Throwing himself down on the bed, he pushed his face into one of the pillows and screamed until his throat felt like sandpaper.

---

Mikey stared at the TV watching an old football game that was replaying on cable, but he wasn't really paying attention. He was worried about the state of his family.

Greg stayed in his room all night, and Barb had continued her manic positivity, cleaning up and singing while she washed the dishes. The tune was something he'd never heard before and sounded like wailing cats.

Once she finished up in the kitchen, she smiled at him and said she was going upstairs to take a bath.

Privately, Mikey was relieved. His wife smelled really *bad,* and despite his desire for her, doubted that he could make love to her later if she reeked of insanely strong body odor.

She quickly went upstairs, and he could hear the water rushing as the bath was turned on. Trying not to seem too desperate for sex, Mikey waited for the football game to end and then rose from the couch. He turned off all the lights around the house and set the alarm before going upstairs.

He took a quick look at the water stain in the living room. It was still there, of course, but thankfully—even with all the rain—it hadn't gotten any worse. The memory of the realtor abruptly hanging up on him re-emerged at that moment, and he wondered why she'd behaved that way. Certainly, Bob and his crew were doing a good job. Yes, it was taking a little longer than expected, but with the mold and the constant Florida rain that wasn't really a surprise.

*Maybe she was just having a bad day.*

Mikey reached down and tugged on his penis. He was surprised to be so horny. The sexual feelings within him had started during dinner (surprisingly, while watching his wife eat with gusto and few table manners). Now, however, he was incredibly desperate for lovemaking. There was, in fact, a throbbing deep within his loins that ached and burned for release. He tugged on his penis for a few moments and then shook his head, wondering why he was suddenly feeling like a teenager.

As he ascended the stairwell, he was somewhat relieved to see that it was dark under Greg's door. He knew that his son wasn't ignorant and knew about sex, but the idea of his kid seeing or hearing him in the act was something he just never wanted to experience. He wanted the teen to linger under whatever shroud of childhood innocence still existed.

Turning, Mike headed to his bedroom. To his surprise, the lights were out, but he could see candlelight flickering against the wall.

*Wow. Barb is full of surprises tonight.*

His penis now fully erect and straining against his slacks, Mikey moved quickly to the bedroom. He no longer cared if he seemed desperately horny. He just needed to have sex and experience release as soon as possible, or his penis might explode in his pants.

When the room fully came into view, he was able to drink in the spectacle. Barb was lying on the bed, completely naked, her breasts and skin glowing in the candlelight. Her hair was still wet and spread out against the pillows like dark webs. She stared at him with eyes filled with desire and lips gently moistened with lip gloss.

Mikey found that he was unable to say anything. His desire was too great, and a haze had begun to take over his mind. There was a musky smell of incense in the air that wasn't entirely pleasant, and it was beginning to overwhelm him with its burning spiciness.

He pulled off his shirt and grasped the clasp on his pants, tearing it away from the fabric. The slacks fell to the ground, and he removed his boxer briefs, which were already spotted with evidence of his heightening passion. In the shimmering candlelight, his throbbing penis jerked and quivered under the load of too much need.

Mikey moved to the bed, and at the same time Barb rose and approached him — pushing him on his back.

She straddled him, and his penis easily slipped inside her wetness.

Normally when they made love, Barb was quiet and timid, allowing Mikey to be on top. She'd use her hands to help move him in a motion that felt good and helped her achieve orgasm. However, tonight was entirely different.

Barb thrust her hips up against Mikey's penis and rode him madly. She shrieked and threw her head back as passion overtook her. Her mouth was wide and twisted, and her drying hair flew in his face as she threw herself back and forth.

Mikey's body was definitely responding. He felt the familiar bubbling up within his testicles as his body prepared for orgasm. He'd never ejaculated so quickly before; normally it took him at least five to ten minutes.

For the moment though, his past sexual dalliances were forgotten and he was lost in a haze of musk, sex, heat, and for once —complete sexual domination by his wife.

She writhed and raised her body, dropping it against his again and again.

Mikey caught a glimpse of her expression, and for a split second thought that her face had suddenly changed, becoming twisted and unrecognizable. The thought disappeared as quickly as it had entered his mind, however, because at that moment a powerful orgasm shook his body. His eyelids clamped down shut and squeezed together while the erotic waves of release crashed over him.

Barb's glistening body erupted in orgasm as well, and she howled as her insides pulsed against him and wetness poured from her opening.

When it was all over, Mike felt his wife tumble off to the side and fall into a heap. Within seconds, he could hear her gently snoring.

He, however, wasn't able to fall asleep as quickly. The whole ordeal seemed like an erotic fantasy that had played out in reality.

Still …

There was something about what had just happened that didn't feel quite right to him.

It felt *dirty* somehow.

When Mikey did finally fall asleep, he felt himself floating into a nightmare—

*He could tell that he was in his room because everything looked the same. But something wasn't right. The air was slow and soupy; weighing heavily on his every move.*

*He looked over to see how Barb was doing and was surprised that she wasn't lying in bed next to him. The sheets were rumpled and looked like she'd been tossing and turning before emerging from the bed.*

*"Barb?" he tried to call out, but his voice was being hampered by the heavy air, making his word sound more like "Blarh?"*

*Concerned now, Mikey did his best to swing his feet over the side of the bed and rise. It was an exhausting effort, and everything seemed dark and suffocating. He tried to turn on the light by his bed, but it refused to work.*

*After a few more frustrating seconds, Mikey stood up. At the same time, he began hearing sounds above him. The noises would alternate from repetitive banging to the bleating or squealing of some poor tortured animal. Despite not knowing exactly where the sounds were coming from, Mikey found himself moving toward the closet where the doors were open. The darkness from within looked like the open mouth of a shark preparing to swallow him whole.*

*He was scared.*

*As he got closer and closer to the opening, the light inside the walk-in closet suddenly turned on by itself. The yellowish-orange glow of the single bulb cast an eerie light over the small enclosure.*

*Mikey looked up and could see that the small wooden stairs attached to the inside of the attic trapdoor were already in position.*

*There were people in the attic.*

*Swallowing hard and feeling the terror of his nightmare begin to consume him, Mikey knew that his body was going to betray him and continue onward—even though doing so might put him in mortal danger.*

*He reached out and grasped the wooden stairs, hoisting himself up and as he took each step it was clear in his mind that there was something going on in the attic the he didn't want to ... shouldn't see.*

*As Mikey got to the top of the short stairwell, he looked around the attic and his eyes widened.*

*There were at least a dozen of Bob's workmen ambling about. Some were hammering boards, others were pulling wood away from the wall. It was a strange sight because each man was working on something different. They were like worker ants methodically moving around each other and continuing their renovations and alterations without any expressions or verbal communications.*

*As they moved back and forth, Mikey caught sight of a small form at the other end of the attic. He tried to get a better look, but there was no need. The figure turned and smiled at him.*

*It was Barb.*

*She was nude and sitting Indian-style on the floor as the men worked around her. But once one of the men noticed Barb looking at Mikey, he stopped what he was doing, and the wooden plank he'd been carrying dropped to the ground.*

*Then the same thing happened to all of the workmen. They stopped what they were doing and dropped their hammers, nails, and other tools. A loud clanging sound reverberated through the attic, and when they spoke, it was as if it was one voice:*

*Then there was fire!*

*Then there was rain!*

*Then there was destruction!*

*You're all going to die! You're all going to die!*

*Mikey covered his ears as the men seemed to be repeating the same words over and over. But upon closer observation, he realized that their lips weren't moving, and they weren't saying anything at all. The voice was emanating from an unknown location and traveling through the air at the speed of sound.*

*And now the workmen were moving around Barb and beginning to touch her.*

*Each man reached out and stroked a part of her body. Some licked her, others grabbed her hair. For Mikey, it was pure torture to watch his wife molested. And then the action began to speed up.*

*Somehow, all of the men were now naked and had grabbed a part of Barb and were sticking their penises in any orifice they could find. One man even started shoving his penis into her ear.*

*And the worst part about it was that Barb was loving every minute. She moaned and writhed and when Mikey could see her mouth, it was jagged, and her teeth were blackened.*

He woke up screaming.

Barb was asleep next to him and remained still and snoring under the sheets.

# 8

## *ROOF & MOLD RENOVATION*

G reg woke up slowly. In the deepest recesses of his mind, he knew that things around him weren't good, and it would be better to remain asleep. But his bladder had other ideas and was pressing painfully, a reminder that humans can't just go into an eternal slumber and expect to survive it.

Groaning, he turned his head and felt something tickle his cheek. At first, he tried to ignore it because his mind was still in the peaceful vestiges of sleep. Then he felt the strange tickling sensation along his other cheek and then—on his forehead.

It finally dawned on the teenager what was happening, and he jumped up in bed just in time to see a slew of mid-sized cockroaches scamper under his pillow and underneath the covers.

"Holy shit!" he shrieked.

He backed off of the bed, and in the process of doing so, stepped on a bug that had the misfortune of moving too slowly out of the way. Revulsion raced through him as he felt the bug's hard shell and softer innards squish and break underneath his bare foot.

"Mom! Dad!" he screamed, while noticing a few other cockroaches running along the wall.

"Dad!"

"Coming, coming," his father's tired voice called out. "What's wrong?"

As his father came to the doorway, Greg was surprised at how haggard he looked. There were dark bags under his father's eyes, and his whole face seemed drawn and gray.

"Dad, there were roaches in my bed! Roaches! I swear, it was so gross ..."

"Relax, relax. Let me take a look."

Mikey knelt down and looked around. He saw one or two bugs underneath the bed, but one of them was dead, and the other one looked more terrified than anything else.

"I see one under your bed. Where are the others?"

Greg was astounded. The other bugs had disappeared, and he could only imagine that they'd somehow found a crevice or crack to crawl into.

*Where did they all go? There were so many here before!*

As thoughts tumbled through his tense mind, his father stood and waited in the doorway, looking like he was going to fall over and tumble to the ground.

"Are we done here? I think I've got a can of roach spray downstairs in the cabinet. I'll go grab it, and then we'll make sure we start paying for a monthly bug service."

Mikey turned to leave when Greg stopped him and grabbed his wrist. "Wait, Dad. We should talk."

Sighing, Mikey turned around. "Son, it's really early in the morning, and I've got to get ready for work. Can this wait?"

"No, it can't. Don't treat me like a baby."

Surprised by the tone of his son's voice, Mikey stopped moving and leaned up against the wall. "Ok, I'm sorry. You're not a baby. What's going on?"

Relieved to finally have his father's attention, Greg wasn't sure where to start so he decided to get right to the point. "There's something wrong with this house and with the guys who are working on it."

Mikey sighed dismissively and waved his hand. "There's nothing wrong, son. Why are you acting so irrational about this?"

Greg felt his blood boil as if he was a kettle that was about to explode.

"How can you say that, Dad? There's roaches in my room, mold growing in the vents, and the roof is all messed up. That Bob guy isn't right. And what about Mom? Have you seen how crazy she's been acting lately?"

"I'm acting crazy?" Barb asked, from behind Mikey.

She looked disheveled, too, though not nearly as bad as her husband. And she was not taking kindly to her son insulting her.

"Listen, Greg. I'm sorry we can't all be at your beck and call constantly, but this is ridiculous. You need to start behaving yourself. I'm getting fed up with your nonsense." And with that, Barb left and headed back to the master bedroom.

Mikey and Greg both watched her stomp away, and then Mikey turned around and gave his son a weary grin.

"Look, I know your mom has been a little up and down lately, but she's just getting used to the new house."

*Up and down?* Greg thought. *I guess that's one way to look at it. He's gonna fucking disregard everything I told him.*

Mikey continued, not seeming to notice Greg's frustration. "We're all a little nervous given all of the issues we're having with the new place. But I need you to please try to make this work, ok? We've given up a lot to move here, and I'd really like us to try to make the best out of it."

Greg was surprised at the tone of his father's voice. It actually sounded like he was pleading with him. Not wanting to make things worse, he decided to back off. "Ok, fine. But if things keep getting bad, can we please consider moving? I'm worried."

Mikey came over and gave Greg a hug.

When he left the bedroom, Greg realized that his father had never answered his question.

--------

Barb stood under the shower spray, feeling the hot water pelt her skin and relax the knots of tension in her back. For the first time in many years, she felt sexy and alive. Life had become hazy and strange, and instead of shirking away from what was different and unexplainable, she was embracing the oddities and darkness of the world.

She knew that something happened between her and the sexy workman from Bob's crew, but she couldn't remember exactly what had transpired. He'd come down from the attic and they'd kissed, but after that, it was all a blur.

The interesting thing was that she wasn't feeling the least bit guilty about her dalliance. In fact, she felt cleansed somehow and filled with a sense of power that was seductive and sexy. She wondered if the workman would come back, and the thought of having him alone again was incredibly appealing.

Sex with Mikey had also been good. He'd been less reserved and worried about his every move and instead had allowed her to take control of the session.

*I guess maybe I'm hitting my sexual peak,* she thought as she ran her hand down her stomach and let it linger over her clitoris, enjoying the feeling of pleasure she was giving herself. Suddenly, though, she felt something tickle her foot and she shrieked—jumping back and nearly knocking herself out on the showerhead.

It was a cockroach. The black insect wriggled around on the floor for a moment, and at first she thought about stepping on it or calling out for Mikey.

But then a wave of dizziness hit her, all of the anxiety began to drain away and calmness began to descend upon her shoulders.

Barb crouched down and almost lovingly took the insect into her palm. She lifted it up and placed it on her skin, then cooed and moaned as it ran over her breasts and down to her mound of pubic hair where it disappeared.

---

"Hello? Yes, this is Mikey Brennier from 4526 Nautica Lane. Yes, I'd like to order a regular exterminating service for the house. Yes, we've had some roach activity. Sure, next week is fine. Mondays once a month? Perfect. Thank you so much."

Mikey hung up the phone and felt his head pounding. He didn't normally suffer from migraines or other types of headaches, so he figured it was the stress that had finally started to get to him. His conversation with Greg had been troubling. He couldn't understand why his son was so frightened of Bob's construction crew. And Barb's behavior? That was another matter.

He thought of their lovemaking and unconsciously reached down and gingerly brushed his crotch. His penis was sore from their rough sex, and he wondered if Barb felt the same way. She'd gone into the shower and was upstairs getting ready for the day, so he'd decided to use the shower downstairs and try to stay out of her way.

It was starting to dawn on him that everything in the house might be a problem. Having roaches in Florida was no big deal, but the mold and the roof—everything was going to cost them a pretty penny, and he had a feeling that their inspector had been smoking marijuana or taking medication that had seriously altered his judgment when he'd given the house a clean bill of health.

Mikey decided that it wasn't worth getting into a conversation with his wife because he was too tired to engage in a long debate or make life-altering decisions. So instead, he grabbed a bagel from the pantry and sucked down a quick cup of coffee. As he was leaving, he could see Bob's van turning down their street.

He thought about waiting for it and then reconsidered.

As he pulled out of the driveway and drove down the street, Mikey looked into his rearview mirror and could've sworn that Bob snarled at him as the van pulled up alongside the curb.

———————

When he got to his office, Mikey decided to try Janice again. This time, when he dialed her line he immediately got her voicemail.

*"Hi, you've reach Janice Walker at Suntime Realty. I will be on vacation for the next several weeks. If you need immediate assistance, please dial zero for the operator, and someone else will assist you. Have a sunny day!"*

Mikey slammed the phone down, frustrated and angry. He was about to try Janice's cell phone number when the operator from the front office beeped into his line.

"Yes?" he asked curtly.

"*Mr. Brennier? There's a man here to see you. He says it's urgent. Can you please come to the front?*"

Mikey agreed and walked up to the receptionist's desk. Pacing nervously in front of her was a man he'd never seen before.

The man was bald and slightly overweight. He was wearing a white buttoned-down shirt that was too small to contain his paunch, and the buttons strained against the fabric, leaving wrinkles in their wake. His entire look was messy and harried. When he saw Mikey approach, he looked up— his concerned face red and glistening with sweat.

"Can we speak somewhere privately?" he asked Mikey without even introducing himself or saying hello.

Mikey didn't know whether he trusted being alone with such a strange person. "Well, first of all, can you please tell me who you are? You obviously know who I am."

The man looked around fearfully. "I'm Don Cranston. I used to live on your street a few years ago. We've got to talk. You're in danger."

The receptionist looked at Mikey sheepishly, and he knew what she was thinking. The man was obviously a bit unhinged, and looked like he could snap at any moment, but perhaps he had something important to say, so Mikey decided to give him a chance.

"Ok, why don't we step inside the conference room over here? We'll have privacy and can talk. Ok?"

The man took a few moments to ponder the offer and then nodded hesitantly, allowing Mikey to lead him to a fishbowl-type conference room that was lined with windows along one wall.

Mikey had done this on purpose, figuring that if the man was armed or dangerous, he'd be in clear sight of people who could help him. He wasn't sure why he was agreeing to talk to

Don, but something in the back of his mind was encouraging him to take a chance. His entire life had become so strange lately that acting on impulse seemed to be the right way to go. It was as if there was an invisible force guiding him down the different paths of fate.

Once they sat down, Don seemed to calm down a bit. He put his hands on the table and stared at Mikey intently for a moment and then began speaking without prompting.

"Mr. Brennier, I'm sorry that I bothered you here at work, but like I said before—I think you're in a great amount of danger. Please just hear me out, and if you don't believe me that's fine. At least you'll hear what I've gotta say, and I've done my due diligence, ok?"

Mikey nodded, feeling his headache continue to pound.

"So, like I said, I used to live along your street, probably about 10 houses down. Anyway, at the time, I had this neighbor who was a great guy. He had this perfect family. Great wife, kids, job, the whole deal. My life wasn't going so great because I hated my job at the time, but this guy Mack was a real good friend. We used to sit together on his porch and just shoot the shit and talk about life. Man, it was great."

Don paused for a minute as if to relish the memory, and then cleared his throat, continuing on.

"Well, even though he was a great guy, Mack was also too trusting. His house was older—kinda like yours—and he was thinking about fixing it up a bit. That's when he met the guys at the renovation company."

Don looked at Mikey expecting to get a reaction, but Mikey just stared at him blankly. He had no idea what the man was getting at, and truth be told, was getting weary of listening to him babble.

"Ok, so anyway," Don continued, "I can't remember the name of the company, but they had a similar white van to the one I saw parked outside your house the other day, and I think they're trouble."

Finally, Mikey couldn't take it any longer and stood up, preparing to usher Don out of the building and hopefully forever out of his life. The man was obviously unstable, and this wasn't what he needed, particularly after the wild sex with Barb and his son freaking out over a few roaches.

What he *did* need was peace and quiet—and hopefully, a long nap when he got home.

"It's been nice meeting you, Don. I've gotta get back to work, so maybe we can talk some other time."

At the obvious dismissal, Don's face grew beet red—yet he remained in his seat.

"They killed him," he said calmly.

"What? What are you talking about?" Mikey sat back down.

"He had the same kind of house as you. It wasn't brand new, and it wasn't old. It was kinda in the middle. Mack, he hired this guy to renovate his house, and it just went downhill. First his roof started to fall apart, and then he had all sorts of things—termites, mold, you name it. I'd never seen anything like it. I mean, my wife and I had dinner in their house before their renovations started, and everything seemed fine, but after those guys started working on it the whole place became like a war zone. And Mack and his wife—well, they started changing too."

"How did they change?" Mikey asked, now starting to feel extremely nervous.

Don seemed uncomfortable answering the question and diverted his eyes. "His wife started getting really weird and sexual. At first, she was always nice and quiet. Demure even. But then we started seeing her walking around the house naked, and I think she was having an affair with one of the workmen. There were so many of them around the house, kinda like a swarm or something."

Mikey thought about how Bob always had different people at the house. He remained silent and allowed the man to continue.

"The house got really bad, and the neighbors on the other side said they were hearing animal noises or something coming from Mack's place. The kids were sent to stay with relatives, and the wife eventually took off with one of the guys from the crew. But Mack—he refused to leave. He just stayed in the house as it kept on falling apart, and then it happened."

"What happened?"

Don cleared his throat, and when he spoke his eyes bored into Mikey's with a forced intensity. "The whole house collapsed. It literally disintegrated into pieces while Mack was still inside it. I heard it happening. It was like a fucking earthquake, and we tried to get him out. He refused to leave, and in the end, it buried him. They never found his wife either, and when the authorities looked for the renovation company there weren't any records anywhere. It's like the company never existed."

Don paused and waited for Mikey to say something.

Mikey processed the story he'd just been told, turning it over in his head. It was horrible, yes. But how was Don drawing the parallel between "Renovators Deluxe" and what happened to his friend? Just having a white van parked outside seemed like kind of a stretch.

As if reading his mind, Don answered, "I know you think there's no evidence that the renovators working for you are the same ones that Mack used, but I saw the guys on your roof. They looked awfully similar to the ones who worked on Mack's house. And there's something else. When things were going bad, Mack called a local realtor named Janice Walker and tried to get her to put his house on the market because he knew that the value was dropping every time there was an issue."

At the mention of Janice, Mikey's heart rate started to increase. "Did she try to help him out?"

Don shook his head. "Not really. From what he told me, she met with the renovation team to find out how long the project would take. Mack said that the owner took her into a room to talk about the situation with some of his guys, and they didn't come out for nearly an hour. And the whole time she was in there with them—with the door closed, mind you—there were all of these horrible noises. Sounded like moans and some sort of animal crying. Totally crazy shit."

The man paused for a moment and rubbed his oily, bald head. "That Janice lady still sells houses, but lots of folks say she hasn't been the same since. In a small town like Oak Shade people talk, you know? And they say after that whole deal and Mack's death, she had some sort of breakdown. Divorced her husband, moved into a small apartment, and kinda keeps to herself now."

Don smiled when he saw Mikey's shocked expression. "I saw in the public records that she sold you that house you're living in. Have you been trying to reach her since this whole renovation debacle started?"

When Mikey didn't answer, Don answered his own question. "Nah, didn't think so. Or if you have been trying to reach her, then I can pretty much guess that she's been giving you the run around. Whatever happened to that poor woman changed her life."

Don pulled a small piece of paper out of his pocket. There was an address scrawled on it in messy handwriting. "This is her address," he said, quietly. "I think we should pay her a visit and try to get her to tell us what's going on. She lives near my mother-in-law who saw her outside walking to her apartment this morning, so she's probably still around. Whaddaya say?"

"Why are you helping me, Don?" Mikey asked. "This has nothing to do with you anymore, and it seems to me like you're putting yourself out there for someone you barely know."

The nervous man shook his head, and when he stared back at Mikey his eyes were moist with tears. "I live with guilt every day. I should've done something when Mack was in trouble. But I didn't. We just watched his whole life go down the toilet, and when he died I lost a dear friend who didn't deserve what happened to him. I'm not saying that I know for sure that what you're dealing with is the same thing. There's just too many coincidences here, and it always pays to be safe."

For the first time since the men had gone inside the conference room, Mikey didn't need convincing.

---

Barb sipped her coffee and watched as Bob and his crew prepared for the day. She could hear the sky rumbling outside, which meant rain. Thankfully, the guys were almost done with the roof patching, and then would have the ducts to finish up.

Barb didn't want to admit it to herself, but she didn't want the renovations to end anymore. There was something about Bob's men that excited her. She felt more alive than ever and feared that once they left, her life would go back to the mundane flow of tasks she'd grown accustomed to.

*You're being ridiculous, old girl. Just let it go. They can't work on your house forever. Just chalk this up as one of those cool experiences in life that you'll always remember fondly.*

"S'cuse me, miss?" a voice asked gently from behind her.

Barb turned around in time to see one of Bob's men standing in the kitchen doorway. He was dark and handsome in a white

91

tank top that revealed a series of taut, bronze muscles. The man's face was smooth with no wrinkles, yet his eyes reflected an age that she couldn't quite place.

The entire result completely unnerved and excited her.

"Good morning," she responded cheerfully, setting her cup on the kitchen table. Barb tried to keep her voice steady and not seem too interested.

"We're nearly finished upstairs with the vents," the man said in a soft voice. "Would you like me to show you what was done?"

Excitement bubbled up in Barb's chest. The last time she'd been alone with one of the guys it had been wonderful (though she couldn't quite remember why), so she wasn't going to miss another opportunity.

"Sure. Lead the way."

The man smiled and turned toward the living room. He walked ahead, and as he passed, Barb caught the scent of unwashed body odor. But this time, it didn't bother her.

It smelled familiar and comforting.

Barb inhaled deeply and then followed the man up the stairs, glancing over at Greg's bedroom. Since their little spat that morning, he'd remained behind closed doors and refused to come down for breakfast. Normally, she'd have gone over to him to try to resolve the issue. This morning however, she felt spiteful toward the child she'd given everything to and who never seemed to appreciate her.

*Little brat. If he's gonna behave this way, then he can stay in his room for a while. I'll check on him later.*

As the workman entered her bedroom, Barb started to feel lightheaded and excited. Even though she could hear hammering on the roof, she felt as if they were essentially alone together, and the idea was intoxicating.

The man walked over to the closet and reached up for the rope, easily pulling on the trapdoor and opening it in one quick motion. The wooden stairs unfolded themselves and waited to be tread upon.

Barb watched as the workman's muscles tensed and strained as he hoisted himself up. Once he got to the top and had stepped into the attic, he extended a strong hand to help her up. She accepted it with happiness and felt a shock as their skin connected.

The attic wasn't the most romantic place given that it was hot, stuffy, and dust traveled through the air in throngs of misshapen entrails. The only light in the entire space—which was quite large given that it ran the span of the upstairs of the house—was a single bulb that hung from the ceiling providing less-than-ample lighting. To compensate for poor visibility, the workmen had set up a network of flashlights, key lights, and lamps.

The entire operation was impressive, and Barb could see different barrels that the men had set up along the perimeter filled with different chemicals to treat the mold. She could hear another workman who was stationed in the upstairs hallway setting up a machine that would help to suck out any dirt that was caught in the vents. She'd seen it out on the lawn before, and it looked like a large wind tunnel with a big black hose running from the back of the contraption into an oversized utility garbage bag.

"There's where the mold was," the man was saying, and pointed down one of the ducts.

Barb had to carefully move around the wooden slats to ensure that she could navigate the attic without falling through the ceiling. It wasn't very secure, so she took her time, and when she got to where the workman was standing, she briefly took his hand to steady her balance in order to get a closer look into the shaft.

She could see green and black mold growing inside the metal walls of the duct and wrinkled her nose at the grotesque demonstration of obvious pollution inside her home.

The workman behind her stood still as she inspected the duct. Then he did something she didn't expect.

He put his arms around her waist and pulled her back.

Heart pounding, Barb didn't turn around or resist. She felt the man's body against her back as his muscled chest, arms, and legs pushed up against her soft skin. Barb writhed against him and moaned softly as he moved even closer to her, and she could feel his maleness harden against her buttocks.

He pushed even closer, and his breathing increased in her ear, causing shivers of passion to travel through her body.

Barb was enjoying her sexual connection with the man, but the closeness of their bodies was beginning to grow uncomfortable. They were so tight against each other that she began to feel slightly claustrophobic.

"Um, can you back up a little?" she asked nervously, trying to reconfigure her position.

But the man didn't seem to listen or care because he pushed tighter against her, and it was at this point when Barb realized that the hardness in his pants wasn't his penis at all. It was a snake.

One of many snakes that were emerging from his body.

And when one found her earlobe, it lovingly licked it first, and then burrowed deep within the orifice.

Barb's screams were muted by the sound of a goat bleating as the words she'd heard in her nightmare filled the air in a breathless gasp—

*Then there was fire!*
*Then there was rain!*

*Then there was destruction!*
*You're all going to die! You're all going to die!*

As another snake wriggled across her face, she could smell the acrid scent of fire and then heard the gentle taps of raindrops at they hit the roof in growing ferocity.

A tear escaped the corner of her right eye and was licked away by the tongue of a serpent.

---

After a quick phony explanation to Mikey's boss, Mikey and Don left the building and hopped into Mikey's car. Mikey wasn't sure exactly what they were going to find when they arrived at Janice's apartment, but he didn't care.

He needed answers, and she wasn't going to avoid him any longer.

They turned down a nearby street, and Don pointed to an empty lot that contained nothing more than overgrown grass and a sign for sale.

"That's where Mack lived," he said. "I lived next door, but after everything happened, we sold our house and moved to another neighborhood a few minutes away. It was too much to look outside every day and see the destruction of our friend's life."

Mikey nodded as he drove. He could definitely understand Don's feelings and no longer thought the man was unstable. In fact, he was wondering if perhaps his family had been the ones making bad decisions hiring "Renovators Deluxe" on the spot and keeping them—even when strange things started happening.

Like the whip in Bob's van.

*Maybe I should've listened. Why haven't I acted on this sooner? All the crazy stuff happening inside the house. The roaches. The mold. What's been holding me back?*

"That's where she lives. Pull over there." Don pointed to a nearby lot.

Mikey parked in front of an unimpressive apartment building. It was small, dingy, and not very hospitable—the walls painted a pea green. It looked sad and miserable sitting on the corner of a relatively well-kept street lined with oak trees.

"This is where she lives?" Mikey asked incredulously. "It's a shithole. And she's a realtor. Seriously?"

Don nodded. "Yep. Told you things changed after she met with those guys at Mack's. I think they really did a number on her somehow. Screwed with her head or something."

*Or screwed her literally.*

Both men were thinking the same thing, but neither chose to say anything. Instead, they emerged from the car just as the rain began pelting them with its warm spray.

"Crap! Let's get under the overhead," Mikey shouted.

Together, they raced to avoid the rain. The building didn't offer much in the way of protection, just a concrete slab that extended out far enough to help passers-by avoid getting completely soaked.

"I think she lives here," Don said pointing to a door not far from where they stood. It had the number 652 in silver painted on it. The door had been painted white and there were cracks appearing against the cheap material. Some of the paint had flecked off and was lying near the doorway in little piles.

Mikey wasn't sure why a successful realtor would be living in such shoddy conditions, and everything was beginning to feel wrong to him. Even the weather was playing on his fears with darker clouds rolling in—bringing heavier rain and wind gusts.

Don reached out and rang the doorbell. A weak twinkling spurted out and didn't seem loud enough to produce a reaction, so after a second or two, he knocked hard several times.

"Hello? Is anyone home?" Mikey called out.

They remained huddled together for a moment when Mikey saw the blinds move. A dark set of eyes peered out at them.

"Hey, Janice," he called out, trying to sound friendly. "Sorry to be a bother, but we really need to talk to you for a minute. Can you please let us in?"

The blinds moved back into place, and the men waited anxiously.

*Come on*, Mikey thought. *Don't hide in there. I need you to tell us the truth.*

Don sighed and started to turn away, when suddenly there was an abrupt click, and the door opened in front of them.

Janice Walker wasn't a model by any means, but she was no slacker in the looks department either. Normally, the African-American woman was well dressed, slender, and radiated an air of confidence that was honed by people who knew their craft and knew it well. Every time Mikey had seen her, she'd been dressed impeccably and smelled wonderfully. Her hair had always been sleek and straight, shining in the light of day.

Now, however, a completely different woman stood before them.

Janice looked like she hadn't slept in days; maybe weeks. Dark bags hung beneath her eyes, which were tired and expressionless. Her hair was unkempt and wild, her clothes mirroring the same feeling—everything was baggy and wrinkled. She was wearing some sort of pajama ensemble, and there were stains along the bottom of her shirt.

"Are you ok?" Mikey asked lamely, saying the first thing that came out of his mouth. As soon as the question escaped his lips, he felt like a complete idiot.

*Of course she's not ok. Look at the woman. She's a disaster.*

Janice gave them a weak smile and backed away from the door, waving her hand to invite them in.

"Sure. It's just been a rough couple of days. Why don't you come in? I'm surprised to see you guys today."

Mikey and Don smiled and slowly went inside.

The apartment was a mess and smelled like stale coffee. The television was on, but the sound was muted, the screen displaying an auction channel selling faux jewelry. Near the TV, the couches and coffee table were covered with clothes, potato chip bags, empty water bottles, and other ancillary unidentifiable items. The floor was littered with trash and dirty clothes.

Janice motioned for the men to follow her to the kitchen where a paper plate filled with uneaten food sat next to a plastic cup and a few dirty napkins. "Sorry about the mess. Give me a quick minute."

She grabbed a trashcan and swept the contents off the kitchen table. Then she sat down heavily and pointed to the other chairs. "Sit. Let's talk. What brings you to my happy home?"

The question seemed forced and out of place amongst all the disarray, so Mikey took a deep breath and tried to remain as focused as possible.

"Janice, I'm sorry we dropped in on you at the last minute, but I tried calling, and your voicemail said you were out of town."

"So, you came to visit me instead?" she asked.

Mikey cleared his throat. "Um, yes. Sorry about that. Anyway, the reason we're here is because there's some weird stuff going on in my house, and Don thought it might be good to talk with you."

Janice sat back in her chair and seemed uncomfortable.

"Go on."

Mikey took his time explaining exactly what was happening in his home, beginning with the roof starting to leak after the heavy rains, and then the moldy smell starting to come out of the vents. He told Janice about "Renovators Deluxe", and about how his wife was behaving strangely, telling him that there was something wrong with the workmen, and then acting like everything was completely fine. He thought about mentioning the strange sexual stuff and the nightmares and decided against it. He was embarrassed and felt like some things should just remain private.

When Mikey finished, Don jumped in—his voice anxious and shaky. "This sounds exactly like what happened to Mack. And I didn't even know all of this before we came in here. I just told Mikey we should come talk to you because I saw that white van parked outside his house and those same guys working on his roof. It's the same guys who worked on Mack's house, Janice. Something's not right here."

The disheveled woman paused for a moment and then rubbed her face with her hands, looking down at the ground. When she straightened up again, there were tears in her eyes.

"I don't know how much I can help you. Since the day Mack Goodman met those damned people, my life has never been the same. I've had moments since then that have been ok, but then everything falls apart again."

Despite the fact that it had taken place more than one year ago, Janice remembered the fateful meeting in grave detail because it haunted her regularly, and as she recounted it to her uninvited guests, she could still feel the terror of that day begin to once again worm its way into her psyche.

*It was a Wednesday during one of the hottest summers on record. She'd been driving home from a showing, the air conditioning in her new BMW blasting on high with pop music lightly playing out of the speakers. She remembered how happy she'd felt that day because her numbers for the month were looking very good, and she was planning to take a special cruise to the Bahamas with her husband.*

*Then like a siren call, her cell phone rang. It was Mack Goodman.*

*Mack Goodman and his wife were good people in Janice's book. Simple, kindhearted, and just looking to fulfill their American dream. She liked them instantly, and was pleased when she'd sold them their house a few years back. Mack had always been easy to talk to and a very jovial sort, so she welcomed the call.*

*"Hey, Mack. Long time, no speak. How're things going?"*

*There had been silence on the phone for a second, and then he responded in a voice and tone she'd never heard from him before.*

*"Janice, I need your help. We need to sell my house. It's a disaster. A total fucking disaster."*

*Hearing Mack drop the F-bomb wasn't something Janice was accustomed to. Immediately, all of her nerves went on edge, and she leaned forward, gripping the steering wheel with both hands.*

*"I'll be right over."*

*When she pulled up to the Goodman's house, Janice was surprised to see the condition the structure was in. There were roof tiles missing, workmen were huddled around a hole in the ground, and all the windows were propped open. To not have air-conditioning in Florida during the summer months was in itself pure torture.*

*Janice got out of her car and made her way to the front door, noticing how the workmen leered at her as she walked by. She made it to the front of the house and was prepared to knock, when Mack quickly opened the door.*

*He looked awful. Normally a clean-cut guy, his clothes were crumpled, and his kind face was now sad and weary.*

*She felt bad for him and hoped she could help.*

*"Hi. Thanks for calling. Let's talk about what's going on, and I'll try to help you."*

Mack led her to the living room where a set of luggage sat awkwardly in one corner. There was a medium-sized hole in the ceiling, and the air smelled vaguely of mold. Everything was dusty and covered in a thin sheen of white specks.

Mack pointed to the suitcases and sighed loudly. *"Yep, she's leaving me. Always thought my wife was the strongest broad around, but she can't take this. And I'm not sure if I blame her."*

Janice sat silently and waited for him to continue.

Mack shrugged his head and took a cursory look around the room. *"Loved this place when we bought it. Can't figure out how it all went wrong. Things are just breaking all around us, and these renovators we hired aren't able to fix it. No one else will touch it. We don't have much choice. Just gotta fix it up and then hoping you'll sell it for us. Whaddaya think?"*

*"Not sure what's happened here, Mack. You had an inspector check the house, didn't you?"*

Mack nodded. *"Sure. Wouldn't have bought this place if we hadn't been totally certain that it was in good shape. I still have the papers, and the things that they noted were small—a little water damage in the garage, some cracks in the roof tiles. That's it. There wasn't anything about a roof that needed replacing or mold. And we've got a serious mess with roaches in some of the rooms. It's the darndest thing. An exterminator came out and sprayed everywhere. Those critters just won't quit. To be honest, I think that's why my wife is leaving. She can't stand bugs."*

He tried to laugh, but it came out weak and strained.

Janice wracked her mind searching for the right thing to say. Since there wasn't really a standard way to handle such a situation, she decided to stick to protocol and remain as neutral as possible.

*"So you want me to put the house on the market?"* she asked.

*Mack nodded and then shrugged. He knew what she was going to say.*

*"You know I can't do that, Mack. There's too much construction going on. Any serious buyer will have reservations about all of the problems you're having. It really doesn't pay to post a listing until the renovators are done with their work."*

*Suddenly the man stood and began waving his hands erratically. "Those renovators? They're part of the problem! I'm not sure when they'll be done and it's all going wrong and— "*

*"And what, Mr. Goodman?"*

*Janice turned to see a short stout man standing in the doorway. He was dressed in work clothes and was flanked on both sides by members of his crew. The two men had olive skin and were attractive and muscular. Still, there was something about them that had her immediately on edge.*

*She felt threatened and unknowingly gripped the arm rest of the chair she was sitting in.*

*Mack hesitated for a minute and then pointed to the stout red-faced man. "That's him. Talk to him. Ask him to hurry up."*

*The man Mack was addressing let out a deep chuckle while the other individuals standing next to him didn't say a word. They just stood motionless with blank expressions on their faces.*

*Janice stood up and walked over, hand extended. She figured that the only way to help Mack was to find out what was really happening here. If the renovators were sincerely trying to fix problems with the house, then there wasn't anything she could do. However, if they were crooks who were trying to take advantage of an honest citizen, she would report them to the authorities in a heartbeat.*

*The sweaty guy who Mack said was in charge took her hand in his and pumped it warmly. It was soft and slimy.*

*Janice instantly wished she hadn't been so friendly.*

*"Hiya. Name's Bob Natas. I run 'Renovations Ultra'. Seems here that Mack is concerned about what's going on with his house. Can't*

*really blame him. If you come into his study, we can lay out our plans, and show you what our quote was for. Every time we turn over one board, we find something else that needs fixing. It's the darndest thing."* He laughed again.

*I'll bet, she thought.*

*"Ok. I think that's a good idea. Mack, would it be alright if I went to talk to these guys for a minute?"*

*Mack nodded his head miserably and motioned toward the study.*

*Janice allowed the men to walk ahead of her, and she followed them. Just as she passed the stairwell, she caught a glimpse of Mack's wife, and stopped for a moment.*

*The woman was watching her with wide, terrified eyes. Her face was hollow and she looked—haunted.*

*Janice waved, and the woman disappeared quickly.*

*For a split second an inner voice screamed at her. It slowed her pace as it shrieked—*

*Don't go in there! You don't know what could happen. Something's not right here. Something's not right …*

*But Janice didn't listen. Instead, she shrugged off the strange vibes she was getting and followed Bob and his men into the study.*

*Once inside, the door shut behind her. Janice turned around, surprised that the door had closed so quickly. She hadn't pulled it shut, so how had it closed on its own?*

*Maybe a draft. This house has open spots everywhere.*

*There's gotta be some wind around here, she thought.*

*Bob walked around to a large desk that housed all of Mack's paperwork. He pulled back the chair and sat down. Then he shifted himself and leaned forward, resting his head on his hands. Slowly, he began to shake his head.*

*"My dear, Janice. It's a shame that Mack called you. Everything is going so well here. Just as we planned. We're getting everything fixed up real good for him."*

The realtor felt his words pierce her skin, but for some reason, she was feeling numb. In fact, everything was starting to get hazy, and she was having a difficult time focusing on Bob's face. It was starting to shift and swim in front of her.

Rubbing her eyes, Janice struggled to remain coherent. "Listen. I think we can come to some sort of resolution."

Bob laughed again, and this time the sound vibrated throughout the room—and felt like it was literally crawling into Janice's ear, eating through her brain, and emerging out of the other lobe.

She put her head between both hands and pushed down, trying to block out the sound. It felt like she might pass out from the torture when everything went silent.

In fact, it was as if she was entirely deaf.

Eyes wide open in terror, she watched as Bob transformed from his current unimpressive state into a tall, hulking figure. His head twisted and shook as spindly horns emerged on both sides of his head. His eyes glowed a deep shade of red, and his mouth was an infinite black hole.

The Bob-creature reached out its arms, and to Janice's horror, her feet began to move on their own, as she felt her body glide toward the evil that waited with wet lips.

When she reached the edge of the desk, her body began to rise, and she floated up toward the ceiling. Invisible hands pulled her legs straight until she was lying supine in mid-air, like an assistant during a magic trick. Then, slowly, her body descended until she was lying on the desk.

Though her mind was racing, trying to figure out a way to escape, her body wasn't listening. She felt drugged and disoriented.

And then her clothes began to disappear. At that moment, Janice couldn't take any more. She closed her eyes and allowed the strange haze to take over and carry her to a place where she wouldn't remember the awful things that were happening.

*When she awoke, the room was empty and dark. Outside, the sun had begun its descent, and everything was quiet. As if nothing had ever happened.*

*Janice was once again wearing clothes, but she felt different—molested. She could feel death inside of her and knew that darkness would forever be locked in her mind.*

"I've tried to forget," she said to her guests, who were both listening intently to the woman's story. "It's not possible. There's no escape. Even my dreams are poisoned by horrible nightmares. I see that man every time I close my eyes. His horns, his eyes. It's all too terrible to talk about. I'm sorry."

Mikey didn't know what to say. Janice's story was fantastical—yet something about it rang familiar to him. And he could see Barb's concerned face looking at him, urging him to replace the renovators with a different company.

And then there were Greg's concerns.

Urgency suddenly hit him with a fierce intensity.

*I've got to get home. I've got to get my family out of there.*

Don noticed the change in Mikey's demeanor and stood up. "Thank you, Janice. You've really helped us here. I knew there was something more to what happened to Mack. It just wasn't normal the way his whole life fell apart. What do you think Bob is? Who do you think he is?"

Janice shook her head and stared at him sadly.

Don could see the tears in her eyes.

"You don't know?" he tried again.

"No. I've thought about it. He might be the devil? I mean, this might sound crazy, but if you spell his name backwards—Natas—it spells Satan."

Mikey frowned. "He told me that his last name was Tansa. Which also spells Satan."

Janice nodded. "Yep. I'm not sure if he really is Satan or something evil that strives to be like God's darkest fallen angel.

Either way, he's doing a pretty good job at ruining people's lives. And you know, I'm not sure there's really any rhyme or reason to it. I think he just enjoys inflicting pain."

Mikey stood and put his hand on Janice's shoulder, giving it a short squeeze. He felt badly for the woman. She'd obviously been through a devastating ordeal and was suffering. His heart broke for her.

"I'm sorry you're dealing with this. Hope things get better."

The realtor flashed a small, empty grin. "There's no getting better. I'm done for. But you can still save your family. Get them out of that house and away from that creature. Bob isn't what he pretends to be. He's evil."

───────────────

Mikey got into the car and stared at the steering wheel for a moment. He wasn't sure what to do. It wasn't like he could go blazing into the house on a white horse and save the maiden in the ivory tower. He was dealing with an evil that defied all reason.

Don sat quietly in the passenger seat and stared out of the windshield. When he spoke, his voice was calm and flat.

"You've got to go back there and save your family. There aren't any special weapons you can use on this guy. I think it's just a matter of getting out."

Mikey looked over at the strange man and felt a wave of respect wash over him. Don wasn't muscular or macho or intimidating.

But he was tough. And he was smart.

Nodding, Mikey pulled the car out of the lot and quickly drove to his house.

# 9

## THEN THERE WAS RAIN

Janice watched as the rain began to fall in heavier drops. The skies were dark and angry, and the wind was carrying the moisture in a sideways direction so that it was hitting the windows instead of just dropping to the ground.

She shivered and moved away from the depressing sight. All of her bones ached, and her muscles felt weak and rubbery. Discussing the past with Mikey and Don had made her current condition feel even worse. Life had become all about avoidance—

—*avoid sleep*

—*avoid people*

—*avoid commitment and the ex-husband*

—*avoid the dark shadows that reminded her of the creature who'd taken her in the dark.*

Her life was unraveling, and she felt like there was nothing she could do about it. It was easier to sit and watch the rain pound on the windows.

Groaning, she stood up and decided that her body odor warranted a trip to the shower. It had been several days since she'd had any water or soap on her skin. The truth was she was terrified to be alone, and the idea of doing anything other than curling up on the sofa was incredibly unappealing.

Still, Janice was able to gather up enough energy to make it to the shower. She stripped off her clothes and looked at herself in the mirror that was steadily fogging up due to the warm spray that was now shooting out of the showerhead.

*I still look good, don't I? I'm not damaged goods. I'm not like him.*

The woman stood and observed her small breasts, flat stomach, and the mound of dark hair that poked up from in between her thighs. She looked fit and maybe a tad thin. Inside, however, Janice could feel a darkness threatening to overtake her mind and spirit. It was the same shroud that she'd been fighting against, and she could tell that the evil ejaculate inside of her was winning.

Turning away from the mirror, Janice stepped inside the shower. She could still hear the rain pounding on the roof above her, and its sound—combined with the hiss of the shower—was strangely soothing. Pulling her head back, she allowed the water to pour over her short hair and closed her eyes as the warmth of the spray embraced her in a liquid hug.

Janice stood there and relished the comfort, when she suddenly felt something tickle her foot. She shrieked and jumped back, hitting her head against the shower head.

"Ouch! That fucking hurts!" she shouted.

She couldn't immediately detect what had brushed against her so she knelt down and looked at the floor.

There was nothing there.

Standing again, Janice decided it would be best to expedite her shower-taking and get dried off as soon as possible. Grabbing the shampoo, she squeezed some of the white creamy froth onto her hand, and started to work it through her hair. And then, she felt it again.

Only this time, she felt a tickle on her neck.

Janice stifled a scream and instead, slapped the affected area. When her hand connected to skin, she also felt herself squashing something that was attached to it. Horrified, she pulled her hand away and looked at her palm.

Bits of black shell and antennae glinted in her hand as water dripped from the crushed cockroach carcass. It was one of the most disgusting things she'd ever seen. It looked like something out of a horror film.

Janice was about to wipe it off, when she felt something tickle her feet again.

Now there were cockroaches pouring out of the drain and starting to spread through the shower stall. Hundreds of them emerged, their wriggling bodies expertly avoiding the spray of water as they moved toward their target.

Her.

Janice screamed and tried to pull the shower curtain aside so that she could get out. But she moved too quickly, and her left foot slipped on the tub. Her body twisted in a grotesque dance and fell forward. She knew things were bad when her chin hit the edge of the tub as she tumbled out, and spears of pain stabbed at her head.

She lay there for a moment, blood pouring out of her ears and mouth, and for a second she believed that death would come upon her peacefully.

Then she felt the roaches as they scurried up her thighs and along her torso.

And when the first one entered her mouth and ran its legs along her tongue, she silently screamed and prayed that the end was near.

———————

Greg could hear the rain pounding against the roof and wondered how much of it was dripping into the living room. It had been days since the renovators started their work, and despite their efforts, there were still dark wet spots staining the drywall. And he could have sworn that there were new ones appearing every day.

He was lying in bed staring at the ceiling. The house seemed quiet, and even when his mother came upstairs, he refused to leave the room. He didn't want to be out in the open with creepy Bob or any of his cronies. Once in a while he could hear banging and knocking, but then the noise would change, and it would sound like someone was chanting.

Greg was afraid.

He couldn't understand what was going on. Why was his mother acting so strangely? And his father was in complete denial; walking around like everything was fine.

Life had gotten totally and utterly fucked up.

"I've gotta do something," he said quietly.

The teenager sat on the edge of his bed and rubbed his temples, trying to figure out what to do. He scrunched up his forehead as he focused on his favorite superheroes.

*What would they do? Fly through the air and swoop down on their enemies? I don't have a cape. I'm just a kid.*

And then something happened. An idea began to form in Greg's mind. It was crazy and would get him in heaps of trouble. Still, he had seen it done in a movie once. When a place was evil, there was only one thing to do.

If it worked …

In order to make it happen, he would need to get to the kitchen unnoticed. It wouldn't be easy because the strange workers were everywhere now and seemed to be breaking apart the house as they tried to rid the ducts and vents of mold.

Greg rose carefully, feeling his bowels loosen. He knew that it was possible that he would be grounded for the rest of his life once he carried out his plan.

*Some risks are just worth taking.*

He slowly opened the door, and the sound of the metal twisting in his hand seemed amplified in the heavy silence that now filled the upstairs wing of the house. The smell of mold continued to linger, but he was starting to get used to it.

Greg peered around the corner and was surprised to see that the door to his parent's room was shut. His parents rarely closed the door during the day, and he wondered if his mother was taking a nap and didn't want to be disturbed.

*To hell with that. I'm gonna go check on her.*

As stealthily as possible, Greg crept along the hallway to his parent's bedroom, trying as best as he could not to make any noise. To his disgust, he could see a cockroach on the wall. It was facing him and looked dirty.

He considered getting something to help crush it.

*Nah. It won't matter soon anyway. Let me just get Mom, and we can get out of here.*

When he got to the door, Greg could see that his hand was shaking as it reached for the knob. Swallowing hard, he pulled together as much courage as possible, twisted the knob, and pushed the door open.

It swung all the way and tapped the wall as it revealed the room inside.

"Mom? Are you in here?"

When no one answered, Greg took a step inside. The room was empty, and everything looked perfectly in place. The only thing that was strange was the smell in the air.

The room smelled *awful*. Like the worst body odor humanly possible.

Greg started to back up when he heard a voice from behind him.

"Honey, are you ok? You've been up in your room for hours. I think it's time for you to join the land of the living."

He turned around slowly to find his mother standing in the hallway. She had her hands on her hips and looked amused. She was wearing an outfit that he'd never seen before.

It was black and looked like it was made out of some sort of leather. His mother was wearing a tight tank top and a mini skirt. She looked bizarre.

In all of Greg's young life he had never seen his mother wear anything so provocative. She always wore loose slacks. Never a skirt.

And never leather.

But he needed to get downstairs and figured this might be his opportunity. Swallowing hard, he gave his mother the most genuine smile he could muster. "Sorry, Mom. Yes, I'm ready to start the day. Can you please make me a sandwich?"

She gave him another grin that he found extremely creepy and nodded her head. "Sure. I think we might have some turkey left overs." Then she turned and headed down the stairs.

Greg followed behind and caught a whiff of his mother's body odor. She smelled horrible.

The rest of the house looked bad too. As he went down the stairs, he could see roaches scurry away and hide under furniture or scamper along the walls. In the living room, water once again dripped down from the ceiling, and pieces of paint or drywall (it was hard for him to discern the difference) had flaked off and were now littering the couches and tables.

The house was a disaster. And Greg had the ammunition he needed to carry out his plan.

Because he'd already decided what he needed to do.

*Gotta burn the house down. Burn motherfucker, burn!*

The place was cursed. He knew that now. The roaches, the mold, the water—it was all connected. And his mother was infected by the same evil that had corroded his house.

The house needed to be destroyed. All of it.

"Penny for your thoughts?"

His mother's voice interrupted his concentration. They were in the kitchen now, and she was slapping a piece of turkey down on a slice of bread. Her movements mesmerized him momentarily with their rigidity. Normally his mother was a natural in the kitchen, but now she seemed out of place and unable to perform even the simplest task of making a turkey sandwich.

"I'm fine, Mom. Was thinking since it smells so bad in here, I was gonna light some incense. Do you know where the lighter is?"

Her smile seemed to waver for a moment, and then she regained her composure. "Sure. It's in the top drawer. Not sure we have any incense though."

"Oh, I've got some in my room. Don't worry. I'll be careful."

She maintained her smile as if it was frozen in place and finished making his sandwich. Then she placed it on a plate and nearly dropped it on the table.

"Here you go."

He stared at the sandwich for a second and wondered if there was something wrong with it. He'd never considered that his mother would actually poison him, but now he wasn't so sure.

Instead of eating, he stood up and casually went over to the drawer, pulling out the lighter. He smiled at his mother and gently set it on the table.

"Just don't set the house on fire, ok?" she joked, smiling. Then she turned and left the kitchen.

Greg wasn't sure where she was going and didn't think it would be wise to wait to find out. Instead, he left the sandwich untouched on the table and started looking around for something that would ignite easily. He was digging through a drawer full of papers when he heard heavy steps enter the kitchen. The teenager froze and instantly knew he was in trouble.

"Hey there," a familiar Southern drawl greeted him. "How's it going?"

Greg looked up to see Bob standing in the doorway. The man had his normal sweaty, beet-faced demeanor and was smiling largely as he leaned up against the wall.

"I'm doing fine," Greg responded. "Summer's starting to come to an end soon, though."

Bob nodded his head and wiped some sweat off his brow. "Yep, it'll be a good thing to get out of this damned heat. So, what're you looking for?"

Greg swallowed hard. He needed to come up with an excuse. Fast.

"Oh, just looking for a phone number of a friend that I wrote down," he lied, "But I can't find it. So, just gonna go up in my room and play videogames for a while."

Bob's eyes narrowed, and his grin seemed to twist slightly. "You shouldn't spend all summer playing those damned games. It'll make your brain rot."

Greg just stared at him with an open mouth, not sure what to say. It was the last thing he expected to hear from someone who looked like he never did a healthy thing in his life.

Still, he knew that now wasn't the time to be a contrarian. It would be best to just agree with the creep and focus on what he needed to do. Greg was about to speak when the realization hit him with the full intensity of a lightning strike.

*He's the originator of all this. Bob is the evil that's making all of this stuff happen. He doesn't look like a villain, and that's what makes him so dangerous. And now, he's trying to get me to align with him.*

As if able to read his mind, Bob smiled, revealing yellowed teeth. "Aw, I'm just kidding. Go have fun. I've got to talk to your mother. Enjoy your day."

The man left the kitchen, and Greg remained in place, sweating and shaking.

---

Mikey drove carefully in the rain, but it was hard to see anything. The storm was now raging and pounding his windshield with firm fists. With his field of vision impaired, he decided it might be best to pull over on the side of the road rather than run the risk of running over something unseen and damaging his tires

*Now is not the time to get into an accident.*

Don had been staring out the window and continued to watch the rain as he began to speak. "Hearing Janice talk about all of those things really made me feel bad about not doing more when Mack was in trouble. You never think that there are such bad people out there."

Mikey stared at the pouring rain, his mind racing. He wondered if Bob had done something to his wife. Barb had been acting strangely, and he'd just attributed it to the move.

*What if it's something else?*

"Don, do you believe in the devil and fallen angels?" he asked.

Don turned to face him. "Yes, I do now. When I was a kid, my folks always dragged me to church where we learned about the fallen disciples and all that. It just seemed like a lot of crap at the time and a way to keep kids from getting into trouble. Now, I'm not so sure. There was something, I don't know … haunted about the way Janice looked. Her whole life seems like it's going to shit, and that's what evil does. It latches on and sucks the life out of you until there's nothing left but an empty shell that's easily disposable."

"Why the houses though? If the men who work for 'Renovators Deluxe' are evil, why do they choose homes? Why not do something more typical like possess individual people? I just don't understand." Mikey shook his head and leaned back in the seat.

"Think about it," Don pushed. "Your home is your castle. It's the place where people feel the safest. Don't you pour your hopes and dreams into that place? I mean, I don't want to sound dramatic, but it's the place where your love, devotion, all of that stuff—you put it all into your home. It's not a house. It's a home."

Mikey continued staring out the window. He knew that Don was right. In the span of a few weeks, he'd moved his entire family out to Oak Shade, and the house represented everything that was good and new. It represented hope and determination.

The beginning of a new life.

Mikey sat up and restarted the engine. He needed to get home.

---

The creature left the teenager alone in the kitchen and moved through the living room. It enjoyed the smell of mold as it passed through the different rooms that were normally inhabited by the humans. The pleasure it derived from the decay and destruction of such naïve purity was always the most intense delight.

It knew that the boy was starting to understand what was happening—humans were always easy to read and probe. That sharp and fearful acknowledgement that all was not right in the world was also an enjoyable element to witness.

Running a finger along the dissolving drywall, the creature thought about how much it had endured since its fall from grace. The heavens had been such enjoyment, but it had stronger desires. It wanted to control more, seduce everything in its path, and feel the sheer enjoyment of its lustful fantasies.

Its constant tendency to seek out and devour more had led to its demise. And it was cast down among the lowest of bottom dwellers to reside amongst the humans who each contained a serving of the light it had once been basking in.

Now, it was no longer a matter of feeling lustful enjoyment or devouring its prey. It had become a constant ache for the light. It needed to feel God's love once again travel through its hardened veins. It hated God, and it loved the Father at the same time.

It lived with eternal torture that was only satiated by the destruction and complete annihilation of the humans it chose to feed upon.

It didn't choose humans haphazardly. Rather, it searched out the most hopeful of souls. The ones who were uncertain and weak in their resolve but who would put up a fight given their ridiculous anticipations.

Sometimes it appeared as a man. Other times as a woman.

Bob was one of its favorite personas because he was an unimpressive fellow who spent time seducing his prey in the most unassuming and ridiculous way.

The creature had long since discovered that most humans underestimated their peers when there was an appearance of weakness. Bob was disheveled and dirty. He represented the lower class of human society and endeared himself to the creature who also found itself treated like less than what it was.

Because despite its punishment, it was much stronger than the humans who it contacted. That made it easier for the creature to extract its revenge over and over again. There were thousands, maybe even millions of humans it had already drained, and still it wanted more.

It needed more.

There was no end to its hunger—to the madness that consumed its complicated and difficult mind. It functioned solely on the need to satiate the burning sadness and emptiness. The affliction was eternal, and hence, it would forever swallow the light and devour happiness. It would continue to destroy and wreak havoc on those whom it chose.

And it chose carefully. It searched for newcomers who were full of hope and belief that life would take them down a positive path. For the creature, those who were the most optimistic and positive were the ones who presented a greater challenge, and therefore, the victory was even sweeter.

The Brenniers were such a family. Such a close unit, so hopelessly optimistic about the future.

The creature snorted. They were weak—the wife in particular. It had already taken her body and most of her soul, but she was strong and still possessed a modicum of light.

As it climbed the stairwell, it found her waiting for him. She no longer had the ability to decipher the difference between him or his minions, and that meant she was weakening. It excited the creature who enjoyed the feel of "Bob." Having a penis and lusting for female flesh was something it preferred.

As the Bob-creature entered the room, it found Barb lying on the bed. It could see some of its spawn crawling underneath her flesh, which rose and fell in different places. She was resting her head against a set of pillows and stared at him with red-rimmed eyes.

The metamorphosis was already taking place. Once the creature had entered a human and released its fluid, the victim would begin to rot from the inside out. Life would turn dark and they would spiral into depression and regret. Eventually, the victim would die via a hallucination, manic episode, or the body would simply give out from the toxicity eroding its every nerve and cell.

Right now, however, Barb was at a very early stage of her metamorphosis where the constant need for sexual attention from her new master was the prevailing desire. And it could see how much she wanted him.

She was now removing her clothes, and all it could see were her rosy nipples and soft, succulent flesh.

"Why, hello there," it said. "Fancy meeting you here. I believe I have something you want."

Barb smiled and rolled around on the bed. "Yes, you do. Come over here and fuck me. Please."

The creature smiled in return and slid into bed next to her. It was happy and ready to get down to business.

———————

Greg watched as Bob left the room. But he wasn't able to move until he heard the man go upstairs. He wondered where his mother was.

*I hope she's not alone with that guy.*

Convinced that no one was going to interrupt him, Greg continued to search for something that would start the burn faster, and found several boxes of matches.

*Perfect. I can set those on fire, and it will help move things along.*

He wasn't sure if his logic made any sense, but it made him feel better about the crime he was about to commit.

Grabbing the boxes from the drawer, he left the uneaten sandwich on the table and took a quick look around downstairs. There were several workmen in the living room, and one of them had made a large hole in the wall. Greg was stunned and just stared at the large gap in the drywall.

"There's mold in there," the man said simply with a blank stare.

Greg nodded and didn't respond. Instead, he turned and went up the stairs, but not before noticing that one of the men who was working on the mold removal had a cockroach on his back.

The teenager watched horrified as the insect remained fixed to the man's back. He considered saying something and decided against it.

*Those guys are part of this. Whatever's going on has something to do with them too. I'm not sticking around to make new friends. The farther away from these freaks the better.*

He gripped the banister and headed upstairs. Once on the second floor, he saw one man pushing a large vacuum contraption into the vent. The workman didn't even give him a second look.

Greg also noticed that the door to his parent's room was closed. He could hear voices inside and was pretty sure that Bob was in there with his mother. Anger boiled within his veins, but he tried to remain calm. He knew that busting in on Bob would be the worst thing he could do.

So instead, Greg went inside his room and locked the door.

Then he knelt by the side of his bed and started praying.

# 10

## *THEN THERE WAS FIRE*

D on shook his head when Mikey offered to take him back to Innovitran to pick up his car. Instead, he repositioned himself in the passenger seat and said, "You can take me there later. Let's go to your house first. I think that would be best."

The rain wasn't letting up at all, but Mikey was able to get down his street. To his dismay, the "Renovators Deluxe" van was actually parked in his driveway and was positioned horizontally, blocking the rest of the space and making it impossible to pull in and park. So instead, Mikey pulled his car up along the curb. When he pulled the key out of the ignition, both men sat in silence and listened to the rain as it continued to fall like iron pellets.

"So, I'm not sure exactly what to do once I go inside," Mikey said, looking at his house. "What do you think? Should I just pack everything up and leave? Where will I go? It's not like we have a ton of money in the bank right now."

Don was silent for a moment, so Mikey continued almost as if he was talking to himself.

"I guess we could stay at a hotel, but what about all of our stuff? And how am I going to get rid of those workmen? If I fire them now, then my house is going to be in shambles, and I'll be left with even more to fix."

"Get rid of them."

Don's words came out so softly at first that Mikey wasn't sure he'd heard correctly.

He turned and looked at the bald-headed man who was staring intently and angrily at the white van.

"Get rid of them, Mikey. If you don't, they'll destroy your life just like they did to Janice and Mack and God knows how many other people."

Mikey shook his head. "It may be as simple as firing them. Or it may be a battle. Will you help me if needed?"

Don nodded. "Let's go."

The men looked outside at the pouring rain, and a silent understanding passed from one to the other. They both grabbed their respective door handles and threw their doors open at the same time.

They emerged into the rain, and after shutting their doors, quickly ran toward the house.

On the way, Don slipped on a stone and fell facedown into the gravel that filled in the driveway. His entire body made a *thud* sound as it hit the ground.

"Don!" Mikey yelled as he turned around and went back to help the man. Water was everywhere, the rain continuing to come down in torrents. When he helped Don to his feet, he noticed that his face was bloody.

"Crap! Let's get you to the house. Come on." Mikey took Don's right arm and slung it over his shoulder so that he could help the man to the front door.

They finally made it to the entranceway. Mikey was about to turn the knob when he noticed that the door was already ajar. The realization make his stomach turn, and for a split second he felt fear once again flood his veins.

Don noticed the hesitancy, and gently maneuvered his hand around Mikey's, pushing the door open.

The men quickly went inside, and Mikey shut the door behind him. When he turned back around, he could see the shock registered on Don's face, and once he was able to get a full understanding of what was going on, he felt the exact same emotion.

The house was a disaster.

Water was freely leaking from the ceiling into the living room. It was running down the walls and dripping in many different places. The carpet was soaked and covered in pieces of drywall and paint. The couches and tables were all wet, and the smell of mold was strong. A trio of cockroaches raced from one side of the room to the other.

In the meantime, two workmen were in the midst of making a large hole in one of the walls, and were shining special lights to inspect for mold. Mikey could see that there were large patches of black muck inside of the wood that he could only assume were mold or worse.

"Holy shit. When did it get this bad?" Don asked incredulously. At the sound of his voice, two workmen turned around and stared in their direction.

The men both wore blank expressions. They stared for a minute and then went back to their demolition.

Mikey heard some thumping upstairs and called out, "Barb! Greg! Are you guys here?"

When no one responded, he felt a chill and turned to Don. "Stay here. I'll go upstairs and see what's going on."

Don watched Mikey go up the stairs and disappear onto the second floor. He mopped his face with a handkerchief and felt strange—a bit like an outsider, but he knew in his heart that he was doing the right thing. Ever since Mack died, he was haunted by their last meeting.

*It was a Thursday, and Don was home with a sore throat. He rarely got sick, and when he did it was serious. This was no exception. His wife had forced him to go to the doctor where he was preliminarily diagnosed with Strep Throat. The nurse had taken a throat culture and told him the results would be back in a few days.*

*The fever was already in full force, and he could barely swallow soup, so the decision was made for him to stay home. His wife worked, so he thankfully had the house to himself—his two children grown and attending colleges in other states.*

*Don was lying in bed when he heard the banging. The noise coming from Mack's house had been a constant irritant for the past few weeks. He wondered if maybe all the pounding, sawing, and drilling had led to his sickness given that he'd been unable to fall asleep due to the work that continued well into the late evening hours.*

*At one point, another neighbor had called the police when the banging exceeded nine o'clock, which was the cut-off point for the noise ordinance in Oak Shade. The workmen had been forced to leave and drove away quickly—the van's engine roaring as they departed.*

*Don laid in bed for a few minutes listening to the noise. Then, after tossing and turning under sheets that were feeling increasingly warm, he decided to put on some shoes and go next door. He was good friends with Mack and could see that the guy's truck was parked in the driveway so why not?*

*Slowly making his way to the front door, Don paused a few times from dizziness. He was sick as a dog, but as his wife always said "he was a terrible patient"—therefore, there was no need to lie in bed,* drink tea, and swallow soup when there was a buddy next door dealing with construction Armageddon.

The sun was bright and hurt his eyes. Don crossed over the small grassy knoll that separated their houses and was surprised to see that a white construction van was actually parked in Mack's driveway. He recalled that the van was generally parked along the side of the curb, but to have it right in front of the house gave it a more controlling look, as if it were settling in for a long haul.

Don finally made it to the front door, and to his surprise, it was open.

When he walked in, he felt thankful to be wearing sandals with thicker soles because the floor was covered in nails, paint, drywall, and all sorts of other ancillary filth. The air was thick with dust, and he was surprised to see his friend sitting on the couch alone.

Mack looked horrible. His hair was covered in white dust, and his clothes were dirty and matted. He wore an expression of pure defeat. A tumbler filled with an unidentifiable brownish liquid rested in his hand.

Don assumed it was Scotch.

"Hey, Mack. How's it going? I'm as sick as an Eskimo in the Amazon. Got this damned strep throat thing going on and figured I'd come over since Dana's at work." He looked around. "Seems like you've got a lot going on here."

Mack responded in a dull, broken voice. "She's left me. She just walked out."

"Who? Jackie?"

Mack nodded. "Yep. Said she had enough. Of the marriage, of this house, of everything. Twenty-five fucking years of marriage, and she leaves me." He gave Don a pained look. "And that's not the worst of it."

Don shook his head, encouraging his friend to continue.

"I think she's having an affair with the damned contractor. Or if not with him, with one of his workers. I'll tell you, she just smells *different. Like there's been some stinking guy all over her, licking her. Putting his damned cock inside of her."*

*Mack dropped his head while Don sat wide-eyed and open-mouthed.*

*After a few moments of silence …*

*"Mack, are you sure?"*

*Don had never been in the presence of an active volcano, but the next few moments would haunt him for the rest of his life, and whenever anyone described an "explosion," he would always remember his friend's reaction.*

*Because right after being questioned as to whether or not his wife was having an affair, Mack stood up and dropped his tumbler to the ground. The alcohol spilled on the carpet, creating an ugly stain that Don had to sidestep. The man's face was suddenly beet red, and when his spoke spittle flew from his lips like small birds taking flight.*

*"What do you mean, am I sure? Of course I'm fucking sure! She smelled like the devil. Like she was rotting. It was the worst thing ever. Don't you think I know what I'm talking about? Or are you just blind to what's happening? He's doing all of this."*

*"Who is he, Mack? Who?"*

*Mack turned his head as if afraid of being heard.*

*Then he turned back to Don, and this time his eyes were steely and unbending.*

*"Leave, Don. Get out and never come back. Things are bad. I'll handle it."*

*And with that, Mack sat back down and looked toward the front door with a vague and distant gaze.*

*Don wasn't sure what to say. But even though he was thoroughly concerned about whatever had Mack on edge, the selfish side of him was screaming—Get out! Get out!*

*So he did. And as he walked out of the destroyed house into the glaring Florida sunlight and then back into his own house, he wondered if his actions were cowardly or appropriate.*

*Two days later, Mack was dead.*

Now, standing in the Brennier's house, he had the same feeling. Evil resided within the walls of the two-story home that he imagined at one time had been very nice. He barely knew Mikey or his family, but this time things were different. He wasn't going to run.

Instead, he decided to go wait in another room while Mikey checked on his family. It didn't feel very good loitering in the living room with the creepy workmen glancing his way every so often.

Don turned to head to the kitchen and was immediately face-to-face with one of the strange men. Instinctively, he stepped back because the fetid smell of the man's unwashed body was overpowering. Privately Don wondered if the man had ever taken a bath in his life.

"Excuse me. I'd like to go wait in the kitchen for Mr. Brennier."

The man shook his head no.

"What do you mean, no?"

When the workman spoke, his voice was soft with a Spanish accent. "We are working in there. You can sit in the living room and wait."

The directive was more of an order than a suggestion, but Don wasn't sure listening was such a good idea. So instead, he decided to wander around the living room, picking up different family photos that were strategically placed throughout.

The Brenniers looked like such a nice family. He wondered why they'd been targeted by the renovators. He ran his fingers over the furnishings, noticing that everything he touched was now covered in drywall ash. He was about to sit down when his eyes connected with something that he wasn't expecting.

A large wooden cross was hanging on the wall.

The cross was crooked and at an angle, and it was only affixed to the wall by a single nail.

Trying to be subtle, Don turned his body so that his back was facing the workmen and quickly plucked the cross from the wall. He then lifted his shirt and pushed the cross down so that it was being held up by the waistband on his pants. His shirt covered the rest of it.

Don carefully turned around to see if anyone had noticed him. Thankfully, the workmen in the living room were crowded around one particularly deep hole they'd created in the wall and were actually placing their arms into it, pulling out piles and piles of black muck.

*How is that possible? These people are like a cancer. They literally cause decay everywhere they go.*

One of the men noticed that Don had a look of disgust on his face and stopped pulling out the muck. Instead, he pointed to the couch.

"You, sit."

Don felt his heart rate start to increase and reluctantly walked over to the dusty couch and sat down. He stared at the workman who was standing in place with his hands hanging limply at his sides.

The man cocked his head and then grinned. It was an unattractive sight given that dental hygiene had obviously not been top of mind for the poor wretch. His teeth were corroded and blackened.

Don planted his feet on the ground and sat on the edge of the couch, not wanting to shift too far backwards and get stuck. He wasn't sure what the workmen had in store for him.

Trying not to be too obvious, he glanced over at the other two renovators. They were still messing with the hole in the wall, but every so often one of the guys would grab his crotch and stroke it for a moment, then go back to what he was doing.

It was bizarre how the man would rub himself, then go back to working, and the other guy didn't even notice.

Then he saw why. The other man wasn't right either. There was something off about the way he looked. At first, Don thought it was the way the light was glinting off of his arms and thought that the sheen he was seeing was sweat that was dripping down the workman's torso. But as he stared and watched, he realized that the man's skin was actually scaly in some places. The patches were black and shiny.

Now, Don began to get nervous. He had one man standing there like a statue watching him, one guy grabbing his crotch every few moments, and a third freak whose skin was stretching and revealing scales.

*What the fuck?* He thought nervously. *These guys are totally messed up. I've gotta get out of here. And I've gotta get up to Mikey. Lord knows what's going on upstairs.*

Don decided to take a chance and began to rise from the couch as if nothing was wrong.

Suddenly, the workman who'd been watching him walked up and was now inches away. Don could smell his unwashed body and unconsciously cringed, disgusted and afraid.

To his relief, the man didn't come any closer. Instead, he opened his mouth and stood there agape, staring straight ahead. Then something started to come out of his mouth.

Don watched in horror as tiny antennae emerged and curled around the man's lips and then began swaying back and forth as if trying to smell his scent. One of the tentacles continued to extend out of the maw until it was finally able to brush Don's cheek.

The contact felt like liquid fire spreading across his skin, and the painful shock jolted him right out of paralysis. Don pushed the insect-man away and raced out of the house into the pouring rain.

———————

Mikey felt bad about leaving Don downstairs with the strange workmen, but he had to prioritize, and right now his wife and son needed him.

He carefully climbed the stairs, and when he reached the landing, he was surprised to see that both the master bedroom and Greg's bedroom were behind closed doors.

*Weird. I guess they both just needed to get away from all this bullshit.*

Mikey thought about going straight to his bedroom when something stopped him. Perhaps it was parental instinct and the need to protect his only child. Perhaps it was because Greg's bedroom was closest to him. He wasn't sure why he turned ... he just did.

Reaching out, Mikey grasped the knob and was surprised to find it locked. Concerned, he knocked on the door.

"Hey, Greg."

Silence.

"Greg, it's your dad. Open up."

He stood and waited for a moment, his heart beginning to drop in his stomach—when the door slowly opened.

And there was his son. The pride and joy of his life. Looking completely terrified and young.

Mikey's heart suddenly cracked, and the realization of his folly fully set in.

*I've been such a damned fool. I was ridiculously determined to make this work—this new life, this new house—and I totally forgot the most important thing. My family.*

Blinking back emotion, he reached out and hugged Greg tightly. "I love you," he whispered in his son's ear. "Everything will be better. I promise."

When they pulled away, Greg was staring at his father intently as if hesitant to speak.

*I can understand this now. I never believed anything he tried to tell me.*

"Go ahead. Tell me what's going on. Where's Mom?"

Greg took a deep breath and told his father nearly everything. He described the insects that were now appearing everywhere, the strange breakfast with his mother, Bob coming into the kitchen and then going upstairs and into the master bedroom. But he couldn't bring himself to tell his dad about his mother having sex with one of the workmen. It was too embarrassing, and he knew that it would devastate his father so he kept that part to himself.

Finally, he admitted to his plan about setting the house on fire.

Despite Mikey's revelation that he'd been terribly wrong about things, and the unraveling of his once seemingly-normal life, he couldn't fathom the possibility of Greg burning the house down. It was too left-field, and he couldn't condone purposefully destroying the property—even if it *was* falling down around them.

"You can't set fire to the house, Greg. I know things are pretty messed up right now. Still, it just isn't right."

Greg's face got red and angry. "The house is a goner, Dad! We need to leave and get rid of all the evidence. Otherwise, someone else is gonna get stuck with this mess. Why don't you understand?"

Mikey reached out and held on to his son's shoulders to calm him down. When he spoke, he made certain that his voice was even and unwavering. Mikey knew it could be very dangerous to panic because he wasn't sure how deadly Bob could be and he needed to keep Greg as calm as possible so that they'd be able to safely escape.

"Listen. I agree that things have gotten out of control, and I'm not sure exactly what we're dealing with here. Let me just go get Mom, and then we'll figure this out together. If you guys tell me that you want to leave this house forever, then that's what we'll do. Ok? We'll pack up our stuff and leave. Does that sound ok?"

Greg stared at his father for a moment. Then he nodded solemnly. "Ok, Dad. Whatever you say. Do you want me to go with you to get Mom?"

Mikey shook his head. He wasn't sure what he'd find, and the last thing he needed was for his son to be traumatized for life.

*Hell, he might already be damaged by everything he's seen.*

"No. Let me go first, and then we'll come get you. Just wait here, and lock the door behind me. Ok?"

Greg looked at him, his eyes full of questions. He loved his father and trusted him even in the face of adversity. But he wasn't completely sure that they were going to be allowed to simply walk out.

He clutched the lighter as he watched his father open the door and shut it behind him. Greg locked the door and sat on his bed, swaying and terrified.

---

Mikey felt the door shut behind him and could feel his heart pounding in his chest. The hallway ahead appeared long and infinite, with the door to his bedroom signaling the final destination. He started walking slowly toward his room while casting furtive glances at the wall and ceiling around him.

There were cockroaches racing up and down the walls, and the air vents now had mold caking the rims of their metal casings. The smell of filth was strong and pungent, and he wondered whether it had been that bad in the morning before he'd left for work.

*It probably was, and I just didn't notice. Maybe I was hoping that everything would be perfect. What a joke. I should have fired those fucking renovators the day they started. Well, today's their last day on the job. That's for sure.*

He approached the master bedroom door and hesitated. All of the bravado that he'd been counting on suddenly dissipated, and his heart started beating loudly at the realization that there may be terrible things ahead. Reaching out for the knob, Mikey could see his hand shaking.

*It's gonna be fine. Barb will be resting, and everything will be fine. Pull it together.*

The knob turned easily, and the door swung open in one fluid motion. To Mikey's surprise, the lights were off and the room appeared empty.

He reached over and flicked on the light, squinting to see if anything looked out of place.

The bed was made, and with the exception of a slight sour smell of body odor, the room looked normal.

Mikey walked over to the closet and opened the door. The walk-in was dark, and the attic trapdoor was shut. Confused, he looked around, and even pushed some of the clothes out of the way, but nothing looked out of place.

Sighing, he shut the door to the closet and was about to leave the room when he heard it.

*Thump*

And then, in the distance—he could just make out the sound of a woman laughing.

Mikey froze in mid-step and waited for a moment. Heart pounding, he stood still and prayed that it had just been his imagination.

*Thump*

This time the thump was louder. He waited for the laughter.

The silence mocked him as he stood like a sentry, waiting for something to happen.

"Hello?"

"Hello? Is anyone there?"

*Thump*

And then —

—a woman laughing in the distance.

Mikey turned around quickly and walked back to the closet. When he opened the door, the light was still on, but now the small door leading up to the attic—was open.

He swallowed hard and then brushed away the perspiration that was coursing down his cheeks. Taking a deep breath, he grasped the wooden ladder that rested against the door, pulled it down, and then carefully climbed the stairs.

Each step he took made him feel like he was passing through centuries of time. But he didn't falter, and when he reached the top and hoisted himself onto the attic floor, the vision in front of him was both strange and terrifying in its almost fantastical execution.

The light was on, and his wife was lying on the floor in the center of the attic. She was wearing a transparent camisole with matching satin shorts that reflected the light against the smooth sheen fabric. At first, she didn't make eye contact and just moved around on the dirty ground, contorting her body into different positions as if she was having sex with an invisible suitor. Periodically she would moan or laugh and lift her hips off the ground, and then she would relax and sigh loudly.

"Barb", Mikey could barely make out the words. "What are you doing in here? It's dirty and hot. Let's go back down and get you dressed. Then we can get out of here. The house is falling apart. We need to leave. Please."

His wife, whom he loved and had shared a bed with for longer than he could remember, turned her head to look at him and snickered. Her eyes were cold and flat; her mouth stretched out in a thin line.

When she spoke, her voice sounded as dead as her eyes, and her words chilled him to the bone.

"You silly man. I love it up here. It makes me feel alive. For the first time in years, I really feel alive. How can you live your life in such a boring, regimented fashion? Aren't you tired of stumbling through your days with nothing to strive for?"

Mikey looked at her incredulously. He couldn't understand what she was talking about but he decided to play along in hopes that he could convince her to leave.

"Not sure what you mean. Don't you like our life? I think we have a great time together. Yes, it's sometimes mundane, and it's not always the most exciting ride. Is that what you want? Drama? I thought you wanted stability. Particularly given your childhood."

Barb's eyes clouded over suddenly, and Mikey knew he'd succeeded in reaching her. His wife's childhood had been rough. Her father had been short-tempered and quick with his palm, beating her when she disappointed him or misbehaved. The abuse had continued for most of her youth and into her teens when the intervention of a counselor and hours of therapy intervened and helped her father see the error of his ways.

His wife and her father had mended fences before he'd met her, but the damage was done. And on their first date, he remembered her clearly telling him that all she needed was stability—in fact, he could vividly remember that day in detail ...

*They'd been eating at "A Taste of Italy," a small restaurant that was conveniently located centrally between their homes. Barb had* refused to allow him to pick her up and instead met him at the restaurant (just in case he was an axe murderer as she told him later).

It was a blind date. Her best friend was going out with his friend and thought that they would make a "cute couple."

Mikey had arrived fifteen minutes early, hoping that he could catch a glimpse of the woman he'd be meeting, and if she wasn't a good fit, be able to make a quick getaway. He'd sat nervously on a burgundy leather couch watching as the different families came in and were seated.

And then he saw her.

She was slender and strikingly attractive. She'd been just as nervous as he was, and when they were seated for the meal, she'd begun talking almost immediately.

"I've had an interesting life," she'd said. "Things now are fine, and my family is close. But when I was younger, my father wasn't good to me. There's nothing more I want in life than stability. I want a stable man, a stable family, and the knowledge that when I go to sleep in my husband's arms every night—there's nothing to be afraid of."

To some men, what she'd said might have been frightening. Particularly to those who were commitment-shy or not interested in anything stable or serious.

To Mikey, however, her words were like a beautiful song welcoming him home. The rest of the date went very well, and by the end of the evening, he was able to show her just how stable and safe he could make her feel.

The memory was a good one.

Now, standing in the stuffy attic, he wanted her to remember that. And he could tell from the way she paused and looked down that she *was* thinking about it.

Mikey took a few steps closer and extended his hand. "Let's go, Barb. Let's just pack up everything and leave. We can put the house up for sale and start over somewhere else. You were right. Greg was right. There's something wrong with the renovators. This house is just falling apart around us. I'm sorry for not listening to you."

She remained quiet for another moment and when she looked at him she appeared innocent and vulnerable.

"You're right. I don't know what I'm doing up here. It's just that I've done something so bad, Mikey. I've been unfaithful. I'm so sorry." She dropped her head into her lap and started sobbing.

The words pierced through Mikey's heart, and yet he tried to push them aside. He knew that she wasn't herself, and whatever she'd done hadn't been malicious or intentional. The thought of her having sex with another man was nauseating, and he just couldn't envision it in detail.

He moved closer to his wife and reached out so that she could grasp his hand. "We'll talk about it some other time. Right now, I really think we need to get out of here. Greg's in his room waiting for us, so why don't you let me help you and … "

"Aren't you the chivalrous type," a voice boomed from behind him.

Mikey recognized Bob's voice and felt every nerve in his body activate. Quickly, he thought about his options.

*Ok, there's only one way out of this attic. The trapdoor. And he's standing near it. This isn't optimal. Since there's no easy way out, I'll pacify the motherfucker until I can get out of here. Then he'd better watch out.*

At that exact moment, Barb dropped her outreached hand. The motion caught Mikey off guard and a wave of disappointment washed over him, but he tried to ignore it and focus.

He turned and looked in the direction of the voice. As expected, Bob stood near the trap door and was flanked by two of his workmen. Neither wore any expression, and their eyes were cold.

Mikey suppressed a shiver and tried to keep his voice light and casual. "Hi, Bob. My wife and I were just going down to get changed and go out to dinner. I'll call you later tonight for an update on how the renovation is going."

The stout man laughed. "Is that right? Well, she looks like she's ready for something—and frankly that's not surprising since we've been giving it to her for days."

Mikey's temper was so heated that he could almost imagine the blood in his veins starting to bubble and fizz. Still, he maintained his calm demeanor and focused all of his energies on figuring out a way to escape.

He cast a quick glance past Bob. It would require quite a tackling job to make it past the henchmen and somehow maneuver his way to the stairs with Barb in tow. If it was just him, perhaps it would've been easier. That wasn't the case however, and he wasn't willing to leave his wife behind—even if she had been disloyal and given herself to the filthy men who stood before them.

*Are they even men? It's debatable. Maybe it would be best for me to just get everything out in the open. At least that way I know what I'm dealing with.*

Bob was standing in place seemingly waiting for Mikey to say something, so he sucked in air through his nose (noting the unwashed body odor that was now filling the room) tried not to gag and spoke.

"I think it's time we stopped playing games, Bob. Just tell me what you want so Barb and I can get the hell out of here. Your services are no longer needed. We're putting the house up for sale, and we'll let the new owners deal with this mess. This is too much for us."

Once again, Bob laughed. It was a mean sound and not one filled with mirth. It sounded mocking and expectant.

*He isn't surprised by this. Of course not. He wanted this to happen. We're fulfilling his fucking expectations.*

When Bob spoke again, his voice sounded different. Even though he still looked like a Southerner, his voice was softer now. In fact, it sounded almost British.

"My dear man. It appears you've been blinded all of this time. Blinded by hope, false optimism, sheer stupidity—I'm not sure which one completely applies to you. Perhaps all of them do. Could you not see what was happening right under your nose?" He chuckled. "I've heard it said that a man's home is his castle. Well then, you haven't been guarding it very well, have you?"

Mikey figured it was a rhetorical question and decided to remain silent. Bob was on a roll, and he didn't want to interrupt him and face the wrath detectable under the reddened skin.

"I'm sure you're wondering who I am. That is a question I see painted on so many of the faces we come in contact with. So, who am I?"

The man put his hands on his hips and took a deep breath. When he exhaled, the air intermingled with a strange haze that filled the room.

The haze smelled foul, and Mikey began coughing. He nearly doubled over from the fumes, but they eventually started to dissipate. When he stood up and looked in Bob's direction, the man was gone—

—and was replaced by something that Mikey couldn't have ever imagined.

When he was a child, Mikey got a comprehensive book on Greek and Roman mythology. He'd made it a point to read it over and over again because he enjoyed the tales and the lessons that were taught by strange yet familiar characters. The thing he'd always loved about mythology was that, even though the characters were written based on fantasy and were ages-old, they still had common traits to the people around him, and the similarities made him feel an odd sense of comfort.

The creature in front of him, however, was nothing he'd ever seen before on any of the pages of his beloved books. It was grotesque and difficult to comprehend at one glance, so he just stared and drank in the features of death.

It had a goat's head with eyes that blazed red. Its mouth smiled and revealed a too-long black tongue that hung from the side like a limp, dead fish. Its torso was human, however, and its chest was covered in wiry black hair. The creature had long hairy arms that lacked true definition and were instead long and curved, ending in claws. It had an incredibly long penis hanging between its legs that seemed to have a mind of its own and swayed back and forth, lifting a swollen head to get a better look at Mikey. The creature's legs were thick and muscular and its feet were large hairy hands that held fast to the dusty wooden floor.

Mikey wasn't sure if the creature could speak, and he really didn't care one way or the other. He was in deep shit and needed to get the hell out. Turning to Barb, he was about to shout for her to get up when his words caught in mid formation. Because Barb was changing too.

She was now lying supine on the ground with her mouth and eyes wide open. If Mikey didn't know better, he would have guessed that she was having a seizure because her lips were moving. Then the skin around her eyes started rolling and jerking.

With horror, Mikey watched as a slew of cockroaches came racing out of every orifice of his wife's body. She was dead now. He was certain of that, but nothing could tear him away from the horrific scene that was unraveling in front of him.

His eyes filled with tears as he watched her entire body darken with the wriggling cockroach bodies determined to emerge from their warm cocoon. Then he turned back to the Bob creature.

"You're all going to die! You're all going to die!" It shouted.

The men standing next to him suddenly distorted, and they too began to sink to the ground as cockroaches of every color, size, and dimension came racing out in flumes. Useless skin fell to the ground in heaps—like costumes that were no longer needed.

Mikey stood in the center of the approaching Armageddon and said a quick prayer that death would come quickly and that somehow his son would find a way to escape.

# 11
## THEN THERE WAS DESTRUCTION

---

D on wasn't an athletic man by any stretch of the imagination. In fact, he could stand to lose a pound or two. That's why scaling the Brennier's house was one of the most ridiculous things he'd ever attempted—particularly in the pouring rain. Not to mention the fact that someone driving by would probably notice him hanging off a windowsill and call the cops.

*Maybe that's a good idea. Let's get the coppers out here to deal with this shit. I'd like to see them go up against those renovators. Put a cap in Bob. Great idea.*

After racing out of the house, Don decided to take a trip around the structure to see if there was another way in. To his relief, there was no one on the roof, so he could move around unnoticed. The outside framework of the house was brick, and each individual piece was large enough to offer adequate foot support for the short climb to the second floor.

He'd started climbing, and despite the rain, was doing better than expected until he reached the second floor. By then, his hands were aching from gripping on to the rough edges of the bricks, and he knew that he quickly needed to find a way in. Sweat and rain poured down his bald head and momentarily blinded him as he struggled to keep from falling.

As Don hoisted himself up to a window, he grunted and said a silent prayer that it was open or at the very least—easy to break. He had grabbed a large rock before beginning his climb and knew that if worse came to worst, he could use one arm to pull it out of his pocket and attempt to smash the glass.

It wasn't a foolproof plan. He knew that. It was possible that he wouldn't be able to break the window or lose his coordination and spiral out of control—falling to the ground in a messy heap.

Grunting, he hoisted himself up once more so that he could see inside. He was able to make out a teenager—presumably Mikey's son—sitting on a bed and watching the door. The room was decorated with sports figures and rock stars.

Feeling hope flood his veins, Don carefully used one of his hands to knock on the glass. It made a hollow sound, and for a minute he wondered if the kid would even hear him. To help his cause, he put his face close to the glass and shouted, "Hey, let me in. Let me in!"

The teenager jumped and turned around. His eyes were wide and filled with terror. He didn't move to help open the window and stood still, hands clutched into fists.

*Why wouldn't he be afraid? He's in the middle of a nightmare. Poor kid. I wouldn't let some lunatic into my room either. Especially when the house is filled with them.*

Don smiled and tried again, "I'm a friend of your dad's. Please let me in. I'm trying to help."

This time, the teen seemed to relax slightly, and he walked over to the window.

Don quickly tried to move away, but the action caused one of his hands to slip, and for a sickening second his entire body teetered backwards. Then he pushed himself forward so that his chest hit the bricks dead center.

It hurt like hell, but it also helped him hang on.

*Whoosh*

The window opened slowly. Don turned his head in the direction of the glass, and an uncertain face emerged.

They both had to shout to hear each other over the sound of pouring rain.

"Hey, are you ok?"

"Yeah. I'm fine. Can you please help me inside? I'm friends with your dad. My name's Don."

Greg didn't respond, but he reached his hand out, and helped Don into the house. It took several pulls but the man was finally safely inside the bedroom, breathing heavily, and thanking his lucky stars that the kid hadn't gone crazy on him.

"Ok, who're you again?" Greg asked tentatively.

Don stuck out his hand and remained in his seated position, his body dripping and aching. He wasn't ready to get up just yet.

"Name's Don. I came here with your dad, but those ... things ... wouldn't let me go upstairs. So I had to find another way."

"By scaling the wall?"

"Hey, whatever works."

Don took a deep breath and tried to steady himself. He was exhausted, and his entire body felt like it had gotten an intense workout. Still, he knew there was no time to rest. He had to find Mikey.

"I'm Greg. Can you help my dad? He's in there with my mom and those people. I'm afraid for him. We've got to get out of here and leave forever."

"I know. Just try to relax and wait here. If for some reason I'm not back in your room in the next ten minutes, don't try to go downstairs. Go out the window and climb down. Then you'd better run, and don't stop running until you can find a safe place to call the cops. Understand?"

Greg nodded and continued to clutch a small lighter. Don found that a bit odd but figured whatever kept the kid calm was fine.

"Ok, I'll be back in a few minutes. And Greg?"

"Yeah?"

"Say a quick prayer for me, ok?"

Greg nodded again and tried to hold back tears.

Don felt bad for the kid. He didn't deserve this. And before everything was said and done, he might be an orphan.

*Not if I have anything to say about it. Better get going.*

He turned and opened the door.

Stepping out into the hallway, he immediately smelled the putrid odor of mold and filth. He also noticed the cockroaches on the walls.

*Ok, that's just disgusting.*

The door to what he presumed was Mikey's bedroom was wide open, so he continued forward. On the way, he looked over the banister to see if any of the men were standing there. To his surprise, they were gone. Instead, the floor was nearly covered with cockroaches.

*What the hell? Wonderful. We're gonna have to step on all that to get out. I guess it's better than dying so we'll figure it out somehow.*

Don was now standing just outside Mikey and Barb's bedroom. It was dark, but he could hear voices coming from above. And the stench inside was overpowering.

Covering his nose and mouth with his shirt, he proceeded forward carefully.

The door to the attic was open, and Don could see a yellowish light spilling out onto the ground. A small ladder was hanging from the ceiling, giving him the impression that Mikey, Barb, and whoever or whatever else were up in the attic.

*Ok, here we go. It's time to kick some ass or die trying.*

Despite it all, Don grinned. He'd never considered himself a superhero or someone who could "save the day", so it was quite amusing that he was taking a stance. But it felt great. In fact, he hadn't felt this good since before Mack died.

Moving as quietly as he could, he entered the walk-in closet and slowly hoisted himself up the ladder. He could hear someone with a British accent speaking, and thankfully, the few sounds he was making were going undetected.

When he was halfway up the stairs, he heard a loud *whoosh* come from the attic, and the entire house rumbled, nearly knocking him off. He held on tightly and waited for the calm to return.

When it did, he took advantage of the mini-respite and pulled himself to the top of the stairs. Once he could see what was happening, it took every ounce of strength to not shriek in horror.

He was standing behind a strange goat-like creature that was surrounded by men who were slowly melting away into a sea of cockroaches. It was the most bizarre thing Don had ever seen yet he was gaining a level of clarity that was rare in such circumstances.

A memory flashed before him.

*It was a documentary he'd seen several years back regarding exorcisms. The victim, a teenage girl, had been the unfortunate victim of demonic possession. In the documentary, the room had been filled with numerous religious people, her family, and her boyfriend.*

*At first, she'd been comatose, her body rigid and unmoving. Eerily, her eyes were open and blinking, but when prompted, she would not reply.*

*Then, the priest had advanced carrying a cross and holy water. He'd sprinkled the water on her body, which had immediately caused her to writhe and moan in pain. He'd put the cross front and center and recited passages from the New Testament.*

*The possessed girl then started to twist her head back and forth. Faster and faster. And then—*

*—she just stopped and sat up in the bed. Turning her head to the priest, she'd shrieked something in Latin, and then the cross had detached itself from his hands and flung itself across the room, nearly missing the boyfriend's head by mere inches.*

Don knew that the cross was a religious symbol, but it was also a weapon. And he had no time to waste. Pulling the cross from his pants, he pointed it straight at the creature, and said one last prayer.

*Please God. Let me survive this. The world will be better off without that horrible thing. Just watch over me and Mikey's family.*

And then he ran.

---

"You're all going to die! You're all going to die!"

The creature was in blissful heaven. It was enjoying the taste of the woman, and could feel its erection grow as it prepared to swallow the man who'd been the source of all its fun. It knew that the desperation and agony coursing through Mikey's veins would taste like sweet honey and satiate its constant burning.

It could see that Mikey was crumbling. The woman was gone already, and without her, Mikey would not be able to continue on. Just like all of the weak men in the world. Mikey would rather give up and succumb to an everlasting hell than escape without her.

The creature smiled.

And then it heard its minions screech. It was a sound they made in unison. They screamed and cried and started racing in circles.

*What is wrong my tiny ones? Why do you fear?*

The pain was intense and immediate as the wood impaled the creature from the back and then passed straight through him until the base of the cross was deep inside its body and had hit resistance.

"Take that you fucking asshole!" Don screamed.

It turned around to see a short bald headed man breathing heavily. The man backed away in horror when he saw the creature's face. The damage was already beginning.

---

Mikey didn't see Don run up behind the Bob-creature, because he was too devastated and focused on Barb. But he did hear the creature cry out in pain and then saw the spike emerge from the other side of the creature's body. Reddish light began to emanate from the animal and fill the room.

"Don?" he whispered. He could barely see or think. All he knew was that Barb was gone. His beautiful, amazing wife was dead.

"Mikey!" Don shouted. "We've got to get out of here. And don't let any of those damned cockroaches touch you."

Suddenly Mikey realized that he was surrounded by the insects and started stomping on them. Greenish goo emerged as he cracked the shells with his heel. Clicking gushing sounds erupted as he stepped on bug after bug.

"There's too many! I'll never make it!"

"You've gotta try!" Don shouted. "We need to get out of here!"

The creature stood in place and felt the searing pain spreading throughout its body. It grasped its stomach in agony and moaned—bleating and roaring like a wounded goat.

Mikey turned back to Barb who remained still on the ground. It was impossible to see her face now because it was completely covered in black cockroaches. His heart bled, and he considered lifting her and carrying her out of the attic.

Don could sense this hesitancy and shouted, "Come on! We've got to go!"

Just then, an insect flew by Mikey's ear. He could hear the insistent buzzing, and it shook him out of his reverie.

It was time to go.

Time to say goodbye.

*My sweetest, dearest Barb. I hope you're able to bypass all of this evil and find your way to heaven. You were a good woman, a good wife, and a good mother. Life won't be the same without you, my love. I will never forget you or what you've meant to me. I'll never forget the union we created together. Rest in peace my love.*

He felt tears well up in his eyes and knew that if he didn't turn around, he would never leave. Instead, he would remain forever in the attic with the filth and roaches and that god-awful goat creature.

None of it mattered anymore. Don was right. He had to get out.

Mikey took one tentative step and then another. And another.

When he got close to the goat-creature, he fully expected it to lash out at him and strike. But the thing had fallen to its knees and was gripping its stomach in pure agony. It roared and bayed and bleated in pain.

"Come on, right over here. Yes, that's right," Don urged Mikey along.

Finally, Mikey made his way around the Bob-goat-creature and grasped Don's hand in an iron grip.

"She's gone," he said.

Don could see that Mikey was in shock. His eyes were wide and watery, and his body was shaking.

"I know. I'm sorry. But we have to leave her here. You understand that?"

Mikey nodded slowly, and tears began to pour down his face. He wanted to turn around. He needed to see her once more.

Don, however, wasn't going to stick around any longer than necessary and gently pushed Mikey in the direction of the ladder.

"Let's go. Down," he instructed.

Like a child, Mikey listened and descended the ladder. Right before his head dropped below the attic, he took one last look. All he could see was the creature shaking and bleating and a round object covered in insects that he knew was his wife's head.

He closed his eyes and continued down the stairs. Once both he and Don were on the ground, they stood in the darkened bedroom and looked around.

Mikey was still unsteady and started babbling. "I've got to grab the photo albums and my checkbooks. There's so much to do. I don't want to leave anything behind. Do we have time to grab my stuff?"

Don took Mikey by the shoulders and stared him straight in the eye. "We don't have time. If you've got your wallet and keys, we should be all set. No telling what might happen. Let's go get Greg, and get out of here."

At the mention of Greg's name, Mikey seemed to come to his senses.

"Ok, you're right. Let's go."

Just then, the creature let out another murderous bleating sound. The house shuddered suddenly, and both men froze and waited for it to stop.

The shaking finally ceased, and they ran out of the bedroom into the hallway. The sound of bugs hissing and humming was undeniably louder.

There were cockroaches everywhere.

They raced across the walls in large dark clusters, crawled around the banister, peeked out from the corners of the carpeting, and could be seen from the second floor, quickly occupying the lower level.

"Yuck," Mikey spat out. "Are those all of Bob's minions? What the hell was he? The king of the roaches?"

Don didn't answer and continued to Greg's room. When they tried the door, it was locked.

Mikey banged on the door. "Greg! It's your dad. Open up. We've gotta get out of here."

Slowly, they heard the door *click*, and Greg's fearful face peered through the opening. When he saw his father, he threw the door open, and hugged him tightly.

"There, there," Mikey whispered into his son's neck.

Greg pulled away and looked back at the men who were sweaty and anxious.

"Where's Mom?"

Mikey looked at Don and then took a deep breath before answering.

"She's gone, honey. They destroyed her. The guys who are working on the house. I can't explain it all now. We've got to get out of here, and then I'll explain everything."

"She's gone?" Tears and pain stretched across the teenager's face.

"Yes."

Suddenly Greg's face changed from vulnerability and devastation to pure determination. It was a strange metamorphosis and caught Mikey off guard.

He took his son's arm and gently tried to guide him to the door. "We need to go, Greg."

"No. Not yet. There's something I have to do before we leave."

Greg lifted up the lighter like a sword and waved it slowly back and forth. "This house can't remain. If it does, then this will happen again. We've gotta burn it down, Dad. It's gotta burn to the ground."

"No." Mikey shook his head. "That's not the right thing to do. We need to be able to sell this place. If it's all charred up, how are we going to do that?"

He reached out to take the lighter out of Greg's hand when Don stopped him. Mikey looked at the bald man questioningly.

"He's right, Mikey. Your house is cursed, and you won't be able to sell it. You think anyone's going to want to move in here with all those roaches? And don't forget the goat creature up in your attic."

"The goat creature? What's he talking about, Dad?"

"Nothing, son. I don't know if I can do this. It means—"

Don finished his sentence. "It means that your dream has died. Let it go. That's what the creature feeds on, can't you see that? It wants you to hold on. You've gotta forget this place. I say, let it burn."

There was another crashing sound coming from somewhere within the house, and all three looked at each other anxiously. Mikey tried to weigh all of his options, but he was too exhausted to fight it anymore. He knew that with a fire, his wife and home and all of his hopes would be lost forever.

"Let it burn," he conceded.

Greg nodded at Don and went into his drawer, pulling out all of the matches he'd found and setting them down on the floor in neat piles.

"In the hallway too," Don suggested.

Quickly, Greg grabbed more matches and assortments of paper, spreading them out along the hallway of the second floor. He was careful to sidestep any of the roaches that were racing along, though some of them managed to make their way on to the litter that was strewn throughout.

The goat bleating started again and was so tortured and angry that Greg dropped the lighter and covered his ears.

Don saw what was happening and grabbed the lighter, quickly igniting the different piles in the hallway, then rushed into the bedroom and ignited those as well. He knew that the bed sheets would be flammable, so he set fire to those.

Then he decided to light the furniture and the surrounding books.

The flames were starting to take hold, and smoke began pouring into the available air space.

"Let's go!" Mikey shouted, and the three ran for the stairwell.

Once they got there, however, they had to be careful to sidestep the cockroaches that were crawling around everywhere.

"Hang on to the railing," Don shouted. "Go slowly and try not to step on those damned roaches."

Each step felt like it took forever, and more than a couple of Bob's minions were squashed in the process. One slew of bugs nearly caused Greg to slip and fall, but his father caught him in mid-slide.

Slowly, they made their way down the stairs and finally reached the ground level. The workmen were gone, and the devastation was overwhelming.

Water freely dripped from the ceiling on to the carpeting, which was soggy from the constant onslaught. Green and black mold had impossibly begun growing on the walls and was now covering certain parts of the living room in a hairy mess. There was drywall and flecks of paint everywhere, and underneath it all, cockroaches ran about in a disorganized fashion.

A large crack had started on the ceiling, and Don saw it first.

"Holy shit. This place is falling apart fast now. We've gotta get out. Head for Mikey's car!"

The trio race for the door and threw it open. Outside, the storm continued to rage. Smoke had begun to pour out of the crevices around the upstairs windows and was seeping out into the rain.

Greg stopped for a moment, his eyes wide and concerned.

"What happens if the firemen show up? They'll put it out. And the house will still be standing. We can't let that happen."

"Greg, listen to me. You can't go back in there. We've got to leave. Let's go."

Mikey didn't wait for his son to respond and pulled him into the rain.

---

The creature was in agony. Even though it had pulled a part of the cross out of its body, the second half remained inside and burned like lava. Its entire sense of being was corroded now by the purity of the Father.

Just the thought made it want to spit, but it could barely move anymore. The Father was to blame for all of this. It had been cast down and turned into this awkward beast because it was no longer in the light's favor. It was an aberration—something to be hated and feared. And now it was dying.

The creature knew that it wasn't really able to die, but this was the first time in centuries that it had felt pain and the dissipation of its physical body. It bleated again in agony and tried to move, but its legs were completely giving out.

All energy seemed to be quickly vanishing, and even though its minions were all around it and protecting it from further harm, the damage was done.

It fell to its side and whimpered as its face morphed from the Bob-man back to the goat. Tongue hanging, eyes glazing over, the creature finally gave in to the darkness.

Perhaps there was something merciful and forgiving watching over the wretched creature after all, because moments after it closed its eyes and entered the world of blackness and infinite loss, a large piece of the roof fell down on top of it.

But it didn't matter, because the creature began to dissolve away until it was nothing but black dust covered in frantic wiggling cockroaches.

---

The fire burned and destroyed everything in its path. Throughout the house, the tiny minions screeched when their bodies came in contact with the searing flames. More drywall continued to fall until portions of the house actually began collapsing, covering the carpets with ash and filth.

Photographs of the Brenniers in their Sunday best burned and curled at the corners as the glass encasing shattered from the heat.

Books and photo albums with years of history burned as the blaze tore through room after room without discriminating. It ate everything in its path and continued on for nearly an hour.

Finally, fire-rescue was called by a neighbor who saw smoke pouring out of the house. By the time the crews actually made it inside, the property was a total loss.

Everything had been destroyed.

———————

Mikey drove into the pouring rain and never looked back. Not once. Everyone was silent, and the storm raged on well into the night.

# 12
## FOUR MONTHS LATER

---

The sunlight cheerfully beamed through the small rectangle cutouts of the kitchen windows. Mikey sat at the miniature circular table and drank his coffee. Greg was still asleep, and this was the one time of day when he could reflect on the past and not be fearful of drowning in sorrow.

He thought about how far he and Greg had come since that awful night.

*It seems like so long ago.*

*So long ago that I lost my precious Barb, and my first life ended. A new story began, but am I really living?*

At first, they'd stayed with Don for a couple of months, trying to make sense out of everything. That had been extremely helpful, and he'd spent hours talking, crying, shouting—anything to help purge himself of the horrors they'd witnessed.

Greg was a disaster, waking up every few hours at night—screaming for his mother. Eventually, the nights got better, and the healing slowly began.

Barb's death went public, and they all told the same story, given that the reality was too fantastical, and no one would believe it: She'd been in the house and gotten stuck in the attic. A fire began due to all of the construction and faulty wiring. When the blaze took hold, she'd been unable to escape and got trapped inside the attic where her poor body burned to death.

*How awful it must have been with all those roaches and dust. To die all alone.*

Upon hearing the news, Barb's parents were instantly hostile—blaming Mikey for their daughter's death. They threatened lawsuits and commissioned an investigator to look into what had really happened.

What the investigator discovered, however, wasn't what Barb's parents wanted to hear. One of the neighbors he interviewed said that Barb had been sleeping with one of the workmen and had been acting strangely.

"No doubt she locked herself in there by accident with one of those guys. She was a creepy sort—that wife of his," was the response given.

Due to the condition of the house, detectives were unable to substantiate anything and eventually ruled her death accidental.

Deflated by the news, Barb's parents gave up on their witch-hunt and allowed themselves to finally face the normal grieving process. They even invited Mikey to their home so that everyone could talk things through and heal.

Mikey politely declined.

Several weeks later, he found a mid-sized townhouse. It wasn't anything like their dream home or a place of grandeur, but it was safe and unblemished.

## Renovation

*At least I won't have to worry about renovators for a while.*

And through it all, Mikey was able to keep his job, and somehow found himself up for a promotion in the midst of everything that had happened. He wasn't sure if it was just a pity play or a sincere gesture. Either way, he didn't care. It was a symbol of his survival.

Greg was still struggling with nightmares. He didn't know how to help him. All he could do was wait and pray that time would heal the wounds that ran deep.

---

*The nightmares never ended.*

*Sometimes the scenery changed, and he was in a different room. Sometimes it was evening; other times mid-day. Sometimes he was alone, and other times there were people in the house with him.*

*The evil, however, was always constant.*

*He knew that Bob was somewhere in the house, waiting with a sweaty face and a wriggling tongue.*

*The nightmare typically began with the creature dancing with his mother. Other times, the animal-man came directly to his bedroom and stood at the door with a blackened tongue hanging out of the side of his mouth, his goat head bobbing in excitement and anticipation.*

*On this particular occasion, Greg was downstairs in the kitchen. He knew it would be best to just go out the front door and leave. That way the creature couldn't get him. But his legs wouldn't listen.*

*They never listened, and instead carried him in the direction of danger every time. He wondered why his dreams never gave him the control he desired. Most of the time, he was at its mercy and felt as if he was constructed of strings pulled by an unseen puppeteer.*

*Not now, he thought. I am going to control this. Ok, take me where you want, and I'll take you head-on. You fucker. You took my mother. You're not going to take me.*

*As anticipated, his legs carried him into the living room. Instead of stopping, however, he continued toward the stairwell. This was unusual because typically he ended up face-to-face with the creature within a matter of a minute or two and then awoke screaming in his bed.*

*Morbidly curious, Greg felt himself ascend the stairs slowly. Each time he lifted a foot it felt like a dollop of molasses was trying to keep him stationary.*

*It was quite an effort.*

*But he finally made it to the top of the landing, and his body was manipulated so that it turned in the direction of his parents' former bedroom. This wasn't the direction Greg wanted to be facing. In fact, it was the one location where he'd never returned—not in reality or in his nightmares.*

*At the end of the hallway, the door slowly opened on its own, revealing a dark maw of unchartered evil. Greg tried to move his body, tried to shift it in another direction—unsuccessfully. And then he was being pushed forward as if on a moving escalator in the direction of the bedroom.*

*Once at the door, he was relieved to find that the room was empty. His body continued moving past the bed his parents once shared, and Greg glanced sadly at all the photographs they'd left behind. It was a life lost forever.*

*As his body continued along to the walk-in closet, Greg began to get very nervous.*

*Is the creature in there? Am I gonna get trapped in that place with him? Oh shit. I need to turn around. Please God, let me turn around.*

*God, however, wasn't listening—at least not in Greg's dream—and his body continued to be propelled forward. Now he was at the base of the small wooden ladder that emerged as if pulled by an invisible hand. The structure stretched out and then lowered slowly.*

Greg's feet moved on their own and began to lift and position themselves on the different rungs of the ladder. He felt his body rise and watched with horror as the attic came into view.

When he was able to process what was in front of him, Greg wasn't sure whether to be frightened or curious—

—because the scene in front of him resembled a still-life snapshot.

The inanimate flames were bright and angry, smoke hung in mid-air, and cockroaches were everywhere. The creature was lying on its side, eyes closed, its tongue resting on the dusty wooden floor.

Greg suddenly discovered that the hold on his body had released its powerful grip, and he was now able to move at will.

*Do I run? Where do I go? Why was I brought here? If I leave now, I'll never know what the dream is trying to tell me. I'm not afraid anymore. That thing wants to tell me something. I can feel it.*

The teenager carefully walked over to the goat-creature and knelt right in front of the grotesque face. It smelled like filth and unwashed animal musk, but Greg wasn't afraid.

And then it opened its eyes.

"You escaped me," it said without moving its mouth. The foulness of centuries escaped its lips.

Greg winced. It was awful—all of it.

And still … he listened.

"In all of my tortured existence, you and your kin are the first to challenge me and succeed. There is something almost poetic in your survival. It is a realization that haunts me in my darkness. Child, you must never return to this place. And if you feel my approach, go in the opposite direction. Otherwise, I cannot guarantee that my hiatus will continue. I will kill you. You will all die. You will all die."

In that minute, Greg was no longer afraid and felt bad for the tortured creature that hid itself under a mask of Southern gentility and hard work. It was a wretched, horrible being that deserved to fall from grace.

When the teenager woke up, his father was sitting on the edge of his bed.

"Are you ok?" Mikey asked.

"I am now, Dad. I am now."

# 13
## *RENOVATION*

The house, now destroyed from the blaze, leaky roof, mold, and insect infestation went abandoned. Mikey's insurance company questioned the cause of the fire and refused to cover the damage, leaving him with more than one hundred thousand dollars in damage.

He decided to not pay the mortgage and the house went into foreclosure and then into auction.

A couple from Minnesota, the Mendosas ended up buying the house for pennies and literally tore it down to start over. They were looking for a simpler life in a warmer climate, and even though the house was a loss, it was so cheap to purchase that they were able to find a builder and afford to start over again.

The new house exceeded expectations and was truly a work of art. It was painted white and was flanked with floor to ceiling windows in the living room. Chandeliers hung from the rafters, and expensive yet simple furniture gave the house a modern, beautiful feel.

Raphael Mendosa was thrilled with the finished product. He knew that his wife, Adriana wasn't thrilled with the idea of moving to a small Florida town. Even though they both wanted a slower-paced life, he feared that Oak Shade might prove to be too slow.

And then there was also the mystery surrounding the former house. When he'd asked the auctioneer what he knew about the property, he didn't get a straight answer. Then he tried to contact the former owner, but all of his calls were unanswered.

It was an unsettling thought that no one was willing to help him understand why the home had been left to wither. He knew from a neighbor that there had been a fire, and that a person had died in the home from smoke inhalation. He wondered if perhaps that person had actually burned to death, which was way worse in his opinion.

Still, the property was dirt cheap, and it was virtually impossible to get such. a good deal nowadays, so he decided to leave the past in the past, and just focus on the future.

He was also hoping that a change of pace would help Adriana get pregnant. They'd inherited a large sum of money that allotted them some time to find jobs and get settled without having to rush to search for income. So in the meantime, he hoped that they could have plenty of sex for pleasure instead of worrying about "what time of the month it was" or "if she was ovulating or not."

In truth, since her miscarriage, sex with Adriana had become very robotic and planned. And their hectic schedules had made it even harder to find the time to be intimate with each other. The relationship had begun to steer toward serious trouble when he'd made the recommendation that they make a move to a slower part of the country where they could still work and be productive, but a place that was slower paced and offered them warmer weather.

At first, Adriana had told him *no*, and that was the final answer. However, after a few months of negative pregnancy tests, she began to change her mind. It was too hard facing her friends month after month as many of them got pregnant.

"It's like they're rubbing it in my face," she'd complained. "I know they're not doing it on purpose, but it doesn't hurt any less."

And so Raphael tried once more to broach the subject. This time, Adriana listened and sat quietly. Her eyes began to glaze over with the understanding that only comes when there is the final surrender to what must be and what will be.

The preparations had gone smoother than he'd anticipated. Money always helped with those kind of things. Given that they now had financial security, it was easy to quit jobs, sell the house, and move their entire lives down south to the warm, humid swamps of Florida.

Move-in day went as planned with the exception of a relatively violent afternoon thunderstorm that frightened Adriana. Those kinds of ferocious rainstorms made her uneasy, so he made an aromatic dinner for the two of them, and topped it off with a velvet red Merlot.

After dinner, they went to bed early and made love gently as they listened to the rapping of rain against the roof. Raphael watched Adriana sigh and close her eyes in a peaceful haze, and it made him happy.

In fact, he was happy in general. The house was wonderful, Florida seemed like a good place to live, and for once they weren't discussing babies or fertility every time they were alone for a few moments. It was a nice change.

———————

The next morning, Raphael went downstairs for coffee while Adriana slept in a while longer. The doctor had told them that a good night's sleep was key to successful fertility, and that they should allow her body to replenish itself as often as possible.

Raphael wasn't sure he believed all of that but more sleep made his wife happier, so it didn't really matter.

The sun was shining high in the Florida sky, and the rains from the night before were a forgotten memory. It was a beautiful morning.

As he quickly descended the stairwell, Raphael hummed to himself. He was halfway down the stairs when he stopped.

*What is that noise?* He wondered.

It was loud enough to resonate over the sounds of the humming air conditioning, but quite different in pitch and tone.

Standing in mid-movement, Raphael waited for a moment, straining his ears.

And then he heard it again.

*Splat*

A feeling of dread washed over him.

*What the hell is that? Is it coming from outside? Is there water dripping near one of the windows? Or maybe I left the sink on. Shit. I'm always doing that, and Adriana is always complaining about how we're wasting water. I guess we're in Florida, so what the hell does it matter if we've got a little bit of water dripping out of the damned tap? The whole state is surrounded by water, and from what I've read it rains here nonstop, so does it really matter if we waste a little water? Honestly.*

*Splat*

*Crap. Let me go figure out where this is coming from.*

He entered the kitchen and started to look around.

*Ok, let's check the sink first. Wow. Looks like I actually did turn off the water. Well, Adriana would be proud of me for that. Hmmm. Where should I look next? Yes, let me pull back the shades to see if maybe we left one of the windows open.*

*Nope, the window in the kitchen looks fine.*

*So where the hell is that sound coming from?*

Raphael left the kitchen and went into the adjoining family living room that had been constructed as a spacious area with sprawling couches and simple, elegant tables.

The floor-to-ceiling windows were vast, and when he looked up it was hard to see anything past a certain point. Kneeling at the base of the windows, he looked around to see if there was any moisture gathering at the corners.

Everything appeared dry.

*Splat*

"Ok, now this is getting annoying," he said out loud to no one in particular.

And then he saw it.

There was a red circle on the vaulted ceiling that was mid-sized. The center was wet and every so often, a drop of ruby red liquid gathered enough steam to drop down and hit his ivory carpet.

*Splat*

Raphael's gut tightened and all of a sudden he felt like he had to make a bowel movement in the bathroom.

*Holy shit. What the fuck is that? I need to go upstairs and see if I can figure out where this red stuff is coming from.*

He went back upstairs quickly, trying not to wake up Adriana by noisily bounding up the stairwell. He carefully checked the two other bedrooms, but with the exception of boxes and the general messiness of moving into a new home, everything was fine.

167

Raphael stood for a moment trying to figure out where to look next.

*Yes. The master bedroom. Something must be leaking in there. I hope one of those fucking painters didn't leave a leaking canister in the attic or something. There'll be hell to pay if they did.*

He walked down the hallway and carefully opened the door, doing his best to not wake up Adriana. To his relief, she was still sound asleep in bed—the fluffy white covers pulled over her head like a crown of clouds cradling her thoughts and dreams. The visual made him pause and smile, momentarily forgetting about his problems.

*Nothing is insurmountable when you have that kind of love in your life*, he thought.

*Ok, I need to figure out where this red shit is coming from.*

Raphael first checked the bedroom. He looked under the bed, around the furniture, and under the boxes. Then he turned his attention to the large walk-in closets they'd built to help store all of Adriana's outfits.

*Damn. Just like I thought. Those assholes left me a present in the attic. Ok, here goes.*

He pulled down the stairs that led up to the attic and was surprised when a dim glow poured out of the opening.

*Great. Not only did they leave paint up there—they also left the bulb on. Wonderful.*

The stairs were difficult to navigate because the rungs had been set too far apart, so Raphael awkwardly hoisted his body along until he was able to grasp the floor of the attic and pull his body into an upright position.

When he did, however, he wished he hadn't.

The scene in front of him was the most awful sight he'd ever laid his eyes upon.

There was a creature lying on the floor, covered in blood. It had the face of a goat and the body of a hairy man. Its eyes were closed, and he could see its purple tongue lying on the floor.

The creature was encircled by a clean line of cockroaches that were all positioned face-forward like an army ready to protect their dying leader.

And behind them, Raphael could see a naked woman lying on the ground. She was positioned on her side and had extended a pale hand with red-tipped fingernails toward him.

"Come here," she hissed. "I'm cold and lonely. He just left me here all by myself."

Then she reached down and started rubbing the dark mound between her legs with two long fingers. She moaned and writhed as her fingers stroked her swollen clit.

Raphael felt himself responding suddenly. Despite himself, his penis began to harden and throb, straining against his boxer briefs. The sensation was immediate and consuming, filling him with an ache that was nearly unbearable.

He began to move around the creature and walk toward her.

*Oh my god. She's so hot and wet. And she's just lying there all alone. I need her to help me relieve this ache that is just building and building inside my cock. All I need to do is kneel down and take her. The orgasm will be so good. So relieving.*

Then he smelled a tremendous amount of body odor. The woman had obviously not bathed in a long time.

*I want her, but she smells. She smells really bad. And Adriana never smells bad. She always has that wonderful woman musk that I've come to love, and she wears that perfume that makes me crazy. What's the name again? It doesn't matter. It smells so good.*

*Wait. What am I doing? I can't do this to Adriana. She's the love of my life. My body's responding on its own, and I'm not thinking straight. I've got to stop this.*

*I need to think about the love I have for my wife. Our life. Our love. No. I'm not going to have sex with this strange woman. Why is she in my attic anyway? She's trespassing! She needs to get the hell out before Adriana wakes up. They all do!*

Raphael stopped moving. And then he understood.

He'd been mesmerized by some sort of evil influence that had tried to make him do something that would destroy his marriage, his commitments, and his vows. It was a force that could destroy his life if he allowed it to happen.

The woman on the ground stopped smiling. It was as if she could hear his thoughts. She appeared angry and ready to scream at him, when suddenly she stopped herself, and just looked down sadly.

"I was in love once too," she said. "It disappeared because I was weak, and he was weak. Don't let that happen to you. Don't—"

Her mouth stopped and remained fully open. Cockroaches began pouring out of the opening and started racing down her neck and body.

Raphael watched in horror as the insects covered the woman's once-seductive body. Within seconds, she was entirely covered in black wriggling bodies.

He began backing away and had taken a few steps, when he bumped into something furry and wet. Raphael's heart began beating like a racehorse.

He knew what was behind him.

Quickly an idea formed in his mind. He decided that he wouldn't turn around unless he was forced to. Images of Medusa and her deadly stare flashed through his memory.

*Will I turn to stone? I don't know what that thing is. It could have the same type of influence. Yep, best to just stare straight ahead and not act too afraid.*

Raphael could feel the creature's warm fetid breath on his neck. It was nearly constant, as if the creature was purposefully blowing over and over again.

"I know you're behind me," he said as calmly as possible. "Let me go. There's nothing you have that I want, nor is there anything I have that you'll be able to get. Stop trying. It won't work."

He heard an evil chuckle from behind him, and an almost human voice respond.

"I *never* stop trying. That is part of my makeup; my being. The Father sent me here so that I could rearrange and take what's been missing. There is such an ache. You are the only ones able to satiate it—even if only for a moment."

Raphael had no idea what the creature was talking about. And it didn't really matter. He didn't care or want to understand. He just really wanted to get out in one piece.

Closing his eyes, he focused on being strong, and on what really mattered. He thought about the love he felt for his wife, the way she looked at him, the way he knew that no matter where they were or what they faced—they'd face it together.

It didn't matter where they lived or where he worked or how nice their house was.

They had each other, and that's what mattered.

At that moment, Raphael felt the breath dissipate as if the creature was losing some of its power. Inhaling sharply, eyes still closed, Raphael turned and ran forward. He didn't know if he would run into the creature or not. He just knew he had to go … forward.

To his relief, his body didn't connect with anything and continued along. Raphael took a few more strides and then opened his eyes.

The trapdoor opening was right in front of him.

Not waiting to climb down, he ran right to the edge—

—and jumped.

# 14

Raphael could feel his body plummeting through the air and knew the end might be near.

*I don't know what the hell just happened, but if I die at least I know that my wife was in my mind, and that horrible thing didn't put its evil hands on me. Wonder what heaven will be like? What's this? Softness? Why does Heaven smell like fabric softener?*

Raphael opened his eyes and was stunned to find himself in bed. Sunlight was streaming through the windows as it had earlier, but now his wife was leaning over him with a concerned look on her face.

"Rafi, are you ok? You were mumbling really loud in your sleep. You kept on saying, 'I love my wife' over and over again. It was actually kinda cute." She smiled at him and looked pleased.

Raphael felt like he was going to pass out, so he closed his eyes and breathed deeply, trying to regain his composure.

*Was it a dream? Did all of it not happen? It felt so real and like I was actually there. But how could I have woken up in bed with my wife if it was real? I can't tell her what I've just seen. It's too terrible. She'd never understand. The stain. What about the stain?*

Sitting up in bed, he looked at his smiling wife, and decided to keep the mood and tone light.

"Honey, I think I left my migraine pills in the living room. Can you go down there and grab them for me? I have a really bad headache."

Adriana gave him a strange look and nodded slowly. "Sure. Not a problem. You're acting kind of weird this morning. Maybe you need the whole bottle." Then she laughed and got out of the bed. "I'll be right back."

Raphael waited until she was out of sight and then jumped out of the bed and quickly went into the walk-in closet. The attic trapdoor was shut, so he pulled on the latch, and the mini-stairwell came down slowly.

It looked identical to the one in his nightmare.

But this time the light in the attic was *off.*

Taking a deep breath, Raphael climbed the stairwell slowly, and when he got to the top he noticed that his hands were shaking as they reached out to turn on the light bulb that he clearly remembered from the dream.

He flicked the light on, and the bulb swung gently to and fro.

The attic was empty and silent.

"Rafi, what the hell are you doing?" a voice asked from below.

He tried not to jump or appear startled. Taking another breath, he attempted to still his shaking hands and not tremble when he replied.

"Nothing babe. I'm just checking out the attic. Since we have so much storage, we'll probably have to put some of the boxes up here. It looks pretty spacious. Wanna take a look?"

"No. And why are you climbing up there anyway? I thought you had a migraine. I looked downstairs, and there weren't any pills anywhere. Maybe you left them in the bathroom. Give me a minute, and I'll go take a look."

Adriana left the closet, and Raphael stood in place a moment longer, trying to let his nerves settle. He knew that there was something at play here. Something bigger than he could ever imagine or comprehend. And somehow, he'd dodged a bullet.

His wife had gone downstairs into the living room and hadn't seen anything, which also meant that the large stain he'd seen in his nightmare didn't exist.

*All the craziness was inside my head. Thank God for that. She can never know. No one can. Whatever was trying to suck me in knew exactly what it was doing. And somehow, it was thwarted. Not sure what I did, and it doesn't matter anymore anyway. Just need to get my head on straight and keep moving forward.*

As Raphael was going down the ladder, the front doorbell rang.

---

Raphael figured the caller was one of his neighbors, so he used the bathroom, washed his face, and put on some clothes to bum around the house in. A cursory glance in the mirror revealed a rustic handsome guy with hollow, sunken pits under his eyes.

*Oh, that's really sexy. Not getting a good night's sleep doesn't do good things for me.*

He grinned at his image and left the bathroom. As he walked down the hallway, he could hear a male voice speaking to his wife. Picking up his pace, he quickly descended the stairs, and went through the living room to the main foyer.

His wife had the door partially open, and there was someone outside speaking to her. He could tell from the tone of Adriana's voice that she wasn't entirely convinced about whatever the solicitor was trying to sell her.

Irritation bubbled up in his blood at the thought that they were already getting visits from door-to-door salespeople.

*We've just moved here for Christ's sake. Can't those people leave us alone for a minute?*

Not wanting his wife to have to deal with the situation for another second, Raphael walked up to her and interrupted the man who was speaking in mid-sentence.

"Excuse me, Adriana. Maybe I can handle this?"

She gave him a look of such appreciation that he almost smiled. Times like these, she made him feel like an absolute hero.

But once Adriana moved out of the way, that feeling of confidence began to dissipate.

There was a man in the doorway who from all descriptions shouldn't have been intimidating. He was a short man with a red face who looked sweaty and unkempt. There was another man standing next to him who appeared to be a co-worker and was also dressed in clothes best suited for construction.

At first, Raphael felt irritation at the intrusion. He didn't want to be bothered first thing in the morning, particularly after such a rough night.

"Look, it's pretty early in the morning, so why don't you come back some other time?" he suggested without even hearing what the men had to say.

The smaller, stout man stuck out a sweaty hand which Raphael reluctantly shook.

"Hi there. Name's Bob Naats, and I'm with "Super Plus Renovations." Sorry to bother you and your wife on such a nice morning. My men and I were driving by, and we noticed that your gutters weren't painted for some reason, and figured we could help you with that pretty quickly. Would cost you less than three hundred dollars if you're interested."

The words spoken weren't particularly out of the norm or outrageous. But there was something about the man's *voice* that set off alarms in Raphael's mind.

He stopped for a moment, and then it all came back to him.

*That's the voice from my nightmare! The voice of that goat-creature thing that was standing right behind me. I'll never forget it for as long as I live.*

Raphael stared hard at the man standing in his doorway. In broad daylight, there was little resemblance between the sweaty construction worker and the goat creature he recalled in the attic. Still, he had no doubt in his mind that the voice he was hearing in his doorway and the voice spoken from behind him during his nightmare were the same. This relatively harmless looking man was indeed connected to his nightmare—he'd bet the farm on it.

Raphael Mendosa was not a betting man, however.

"I'm sorry. We're not interested in any renovations right now. Thanks for coming by."

He grasped the handle and began to close the door.

Bob put his foot out, momentarily blocking Raphael's ability to completely shut him out.

"Yes?" Raphael asked, trying to seem rushed and irritated and desperately hoping that the man wouldn't be able to read his mind—discovering the fear that lurked there.

"Not trying to be pushy, but you didn't really give me a chance to describe what kinds of renovations we can do. My crew can handle painting, roof repairs, mold, insects, whatever you need. If you just give me a chance to look around, we can make sure your new home is spick and span."

"How did you know my house was new?" Raphael asked, raising his eyebrow.

For a split second, Bob seemed to hesitate, and there was a dark flicker in his eye. Then it disappeared, and he was once again congenial as ever. The man next to him remained quiet and didn't say a word.

"I've been in these parts awhile and saw what happened to this house before. Y'all have done a great job getting everything redone. Can I take a look around?"

*Wow, he's really trying hard. I'd bet he'd just love to take a tour.*

"Now really isn't a good time. We've got a lot of things we have to do."

"Are you sure? It'd be good to see the old place all done up."

Raphael decided to push just one last time for good measure. He knew it probably wasn't in his best interest, but he couldn't help it. There was something so disgustingly shallow about the man—like a sheer layer of a costume that was hiding the malformed and wretched thing underneath.

He tread carefully at first.

"Oh, so you've been in the house before?"

Bob smiled and took the opening wholeheartedly, "Why, yes, we have. We had to work on a number of problems the former homeowner was dealing with. You see, he bought this house when it was quite old and didn't really have a good inspection. Once he moved in, he discovered all sorts of problems, and we came in and tried to help him. Funny thing is, he burned the place down before we could finish the repairs we'd started. Damn shame."

"Funny he missed all of those problems when he moved in, isn't it?"

Bob's smile wavered and he responded curtly, "The guy wasn't exactly the most thorough of people. It doesn't surprise me that he didn't catch a lot of problems in the beginning. And once he knew what needed to be fixed, he brought us in. Not sure why he decided to throw in the towel. Guess he ran out of money."

"And killed his wife in the process?"

This time, Bob's eyes flashed with anger. "Don't believe everything you hear. That woman didn't kill herself. Her husband torched the place and took off. Neighbors saw everything."

*Yes, they did, Bob. And wouldn't you know it, I've already spoken to all of them.*

Raphael took a deep breath and readied himself. He wasn't a man of great physical strength, however, his mind had never been stronger.

"Bob, as much as I'd like to give you a tour of our house, it just isn't in the cards right now. Or ever. And if you come back, you can expect the same answer from me. You aren't welcome."

He pushed Bob's foot out of the doorway.

"And our attic? It's off limits too. Find some other place to hang out with your insects. They aren't welcome here."

He slammed the door shut before another word could be spoken.

———

Raphael stood and stared at the door for a moment. He was shaking and sweat glistened on his forehead.

"You weren't very nice to them," his wife said, walking up behind him.

"They were scumbags. Leeches. Sorry you had to deal with them."

Adriana laughed. "Wow, you really didn't like those men. When you were upstairs, he rang the doorbell, and I tried to get rid of him. The guy just wouldn't take no for an answer."

Raphael walked over to the window. He could see a white van parked along the curb with the words "Renovators" painted on the side.

Bob and his workmen were standing near the van, staring at the house. Bob looked furious and was holding something in his hand that resembled a whip. He was glaring straight at Raphael as if he could see from a great distance through the window and into the house.

Raphael moved out of sight, taken aback at the man's ferocity.

"Are you ok?" asked Adriana.

"Yeah, hang on."

Raphael slowly moved toward the window and looked out once more.

This time, Bob and his passenger were back in the van and were pulling away from the curb. The van slowly moved away from the sidewalk.

Raphael ran outside, thinking it might be good to get the license plate number and report the company to the police — citing harassment.

The heat from the Florida sun beat down on him as he raced down the driveway and into the street hoping to catch a glimpse of the license plate.

The van drove along on the road and then ... disappeared into thin air.

A blast of hot wind swept through and hit Raphael in the face head on, almost knocking him over.

He exhaled sharply and stumbled back, still staring in the direction of where the van had been headed.

*It's gone. It's gone and will never come back. I'm safe. Adriana's safe. Hell, the whole damned neighborhood is probably better off. Good riddance.*

"Wow, it's hot out here. What the hell are you doing?" Adriana asked, a twinge of irritation in her voice.

"Was just making sure that guy left us alone. He's gone. We're safe now."

Together they stood in the middle of the street, watching as the warm wind blew leaves along the vacant asphalt.

The next month, Adriana found out that she was pregnant.

# ABOUT THE AUTHOR

Sara Brooke is an Amazon bestselling author of horror, paranormal romance, and suspense fiction.

A lifelong avid reader of all things scary, Sara's childhood dream was to write books that make readers sleep with their lights on. She hopes that isn't too troubling for the thousands of readers worldwide who have purchased her books.

Sara has been published alongside horror legends Clive Barker and John Carpenter. She has written ten novels, and numerous novellas and short stories.

Sara resides in beautiful South Florida. She can be reached via her website at www.sarabrooke.com. Sara welcomes feedback and questions from readers.

## Bibliography

**Novels**
Cursed Casino

Gardens of Babylon
Kransen House
Renovation
Still Lake
Sunken Park
The Bloodmane Chronicles
The Inn and Other Dark Tales
The Island
The Zyne Project

**Novellas and Short Stories**
Bathroom (Short Story in Madhouse Anthology)
Doug (Short Story)
Famine (Short Story in Anthology including stories from Clive
Barker & John Carpenter – currently in film development)
Ghost Swim (Short Story)
Mad Monkey King (Short Story)
Stairwell (Short Story)
The Bed (novella)
The Field (Short Story)
Vicious Circle (Short Story in Vicious Circle Anthology)

Curious about other Crossroad Press books? Stop by our
website: http://crossroadpress.com
We offer quality writing
in digital, audio, and print formats.

Subscribe to our newsletter on the website homepage and
receive a free eBook.

www.ingramcontent.com/pod-product-compliance
Lightning Source LLC
Chambersburg PA
CBHW022113170626
46808CB00002B/713